advance praise for

Eat Your Heart Out

"Sex, violence, and horror combine in a ridiculously entertaining novella of lesbians and zombies... [A] no-holds-barred action-packed romp, filled with rich descriptions, detailed sensory input, sexy flirting, and zombie fighting in the best cult tradition. Ingram has a keen ear for dialogue and believable characters, and this punchy, raunchy story would make a great grindhouse film."

—*Publishers Weekly* (starred review)

"Dayna Ingram is an irrepressible and shameless comedienne of the Dark Side. Read *Eat Your Heart Out* if you appreciate suspense, horror, sex, humor, and of course zombies."

—Maxine Chernoff, author of *A House in Summer*

"A smart, sassy and sexy romp through the zombie apocalypse, with just the right mix of gore and humor and kick-ass heroines. Devin and Renni will grab your imagination and then kick you in the crotch if you get in their way. Pulp at its best—it will leave you wanting a movie version, a graphic novel, the indie soundtrack and a dozen thrilling sequels."

—Sandra McDonald, author of *Diana Comet & Other Improbable Stories*

"This book is a double scoop of melt-in-your-mouth guts-and-brains-flavored ice cream with a pop culture cherry on top, in a word: yummy! *Eat Your Heart Out* announces with a guttural zombie howl that Dayna Ingram is a talent to watch out for."

—Tom Cardamone, author of *Pumpkin Teeth*

"Guts, guns, girls and glory—as zombies overrun a small Midwestern town, plucky protagonist Devin battles her way through the nomming undead not only to safety, but to the heart of her beautiful, tough-as-nails companion, B-horror movie star Renni Ramirez. *Eat Your Heart Out* is a sly, clever, sexy and thoroughly original take on zombies, with a wink and nod toward the cultural power of Hollywood, and our endless fascination with the undead. A deliciously fun read that will leave readers voraciously clamoring for more."

—Livia Llewellyn, author of *Engines of Desire*

"*Eat Your Heart Out* is a wildly inventive, laugh out loud, deliciously sexy zombie romp—with lesbians. Really, what more do you need?"

—JoSelle Vanderhooft, editor of *Steam-Powered I & II: Lesbian Steampunk Stories*

Eat Your Heart Out

a novella by

DAYNA INGRAM

EAT YOUR HEART OUT

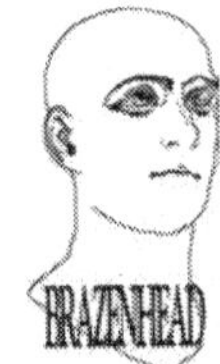

eat your heart out

A BrazenHead novella, published in 2011 by Lethe Press, Inc.
118 Heritage Avenue • Maple Shade, NJ 08052-3018
sentenceandparagraph.com/brazenhead
www.lethepressbooks.com • lethepress@aol.com
ISBN: 1-59021-333-5
ISBN-13: 978-1-59021-333-9

This book is a work of fiction. Any references to historical events, real people, or real locales are used fictitiously. Other names, characters, places, and incidents are products of the author's imagination and any resemblance to actual locales, events, or persons, living or dead, is entirely coincidental.

BrazenHead books are selected, edited, and designed by Alex Jeffers, brazenhead@sentenceandparagraph.com.
Set in Jenson, Water Street, and UglyQua.
Cover photos:
"Packing Heat" Nina Shannon / "Rotten Hand" Gerard Galvan.

Library of Congress Cataloging-in-Publication Data
Ingram, Dayna.
Eat your heart out : a novella / Dayna Ingram.
p. cm.
ISBN 978-1-59021-333-9 (pbk. : alk. paper)
1. Lesbians--Fiction. 2. Zombies--Fiction. I. Title.
PS3609.N4686E28 2011
813'.6--dc23

2011039634

For Michelle Rodriguez

Acknowledgments

Special thanks go out to my sister Erin, for reading everything I write and always being gracious with her feedback; to my Dad, for his encouragement and support; to Amy Campbell and Amber Froncillo, for their long-distance writerly companionship; and to Alex Jeffers, for overcoming his intense dislike of first-person present-tense narration and zombies, and taking a chance on me.

Chapter 1

All's Dead That Ends Dead

MY FIRST REAL-LIFE ZOMBIE ENCOUNTER IS A PRETTY low-key affair, considering I don't even realize at the time what I'm dealing with. I'm under a lot of pressure from all sides this morning: I have to be in early at Ashbee's Furniture Outlet to shadow the assistant manager so he can teach me how to open; I've actually been shadowing Biff for a week now and think I've got it down but the manual says every new shift leader needs two weeks of opening training and two weeks of closing training, and there is no wriggle room with Biff Tipping. So I'm already in a hurry when my girlfriend asks me to stop by the coffee shop and get her usual breakfast—a double-mocha Frappuccino thing that I'm pretty sure can't legally be called coffee. I can't say no to her because, as she reminds me, she did go down on me the previous night for the first time in two months. I owe her. She has to get to work too, so I am really under a time crunch. The coffee shop is of course packed so early in the morning, and while in line I watch the minute hand of my wristwatch tick past the one, and Biff calls.

"Ten minutes late and you won't get paid for the hour," he says.

"Okay, I'll see you at nine then."

"Don't be a smartass, Devin. Just get here."

When it is my turn up at the counter I decide to go ahead and get a treat for Biff and the others who'll be opening today, Cherry and Brad. I don't know what they like so I just get three extra coffees and some sugar and powdered cream on the side. I'm trying to shuffle all of this out the door when my phone starts buzzing. I can't maneuver my hand into my pocket very smoothly while carrying the tray of coffees and holding the door open. I'm a graceless swan, fumbling around and apologizing to the line I'm holding up in front of and behind me. Finally I get the phone out and flip it to my ear, and that's when it happens. The real-life zombie.

Only I don't see him as a zombie, just an old drunk dude. He's walking like he has a limp in both legs, keeping his eyes to the ground so all I can see is the skin along the part in his stringy brown hair, scabbed over like his scalp has rejected hair plugs. He's moaning kind of low, the way you do when you just wake up and can't quite face the day even though you know you gotta, and everyone in line just kind of moves out of his way without even needing to be touched. By the time he reaches me I can tell why everyone is backing off: he reeks, like cottage cheese in the underwear of a two-dollar hooker left out in the sun (the underwear, not the hooker, but probably the same odor would result).

"Excuse me," I say, trying to lean up against the door to allow him access. For a brief second he looks up at me and I can see the nothing in his eyes that I mistake for a drunken stupor. He stops abruptly and then kind of slowly bends toward me, but someone elbows me in the back and I stumble past him, out the door and into the waiting line of people.

"Watch it!" someone yells.

"Devin? Are you there? Devin!" my girlfriend squawks into my ear.

"Yeah, yeah, I'm here. Sorry." I push away from the coffee-shop entrance, distantly registering a surprised yelp behind me and a gruff response, which I assume signals the start of some sort of altercation between one patron and another, perhaps the old drunk guy.

"Devin, where the hell are you? I'm going to be late." My girlfriend's name is Carmelle Soufflé, like the dessert. She's never forgiven her parents for this but still hasn't legally changed it, so I can't feel too bad for her. We met during college, before I dropped out, when she was working at a strip club and going by the stage name Caramel Apple. Sometimes I slip up and accidentally call her Caramel instead of Carmelle and she stops speaking to me until I make some grand gesture of apology, which usually involves a significant portion of my meager paycheck.

"I'll be there in two minutes, honey," I tell her. Our apartment is just on the other side of the block. This coffee shop is literally our backyard, but we're separated by a fence so I have to walk around the whole block. We live above a small independently owned pet shop that only sells supplies for reptiles and fish, but still has kittens and puppies painted on their windows. I've only been inside once and there weren't any customers and everything smelled like week-old marijuana. I think the whole store's a front for a mild drug cartel, but no one wants to hear my theories.

Carmelle almost knocks into me as she's rushing out the door. "Jesus, you startled me!"

She doesn't strip anymore, but she does work at a sex shop so she still wears kind of revealing clothes. I don't mind because I trust her but it's late September and she's still not wearing sleeves or pants so sometimes I get concerned for her health.

"You're not gonna wear the jacket I bought you?" I ask her. It's barely a jacket; it's very light fabric that only goes to her midriff and purposely doesn't button so her cleavage is still visible.

"Ah, baby, come on, don't start with me." She plucks her frozen mocha drink from the tray and presses her chest against mine to lean in and kiss me on the nose. "Don't wait up."

I watch her bound down the outer staircase to the sidewalk, taking a little leap off the final step, sipping at her drink as she saunters down the block. We haven't said "I love you" yet, even though we've been living together for four months and dating for over a year. She's the only girl I've ever been with and I've been kind of following her lead, so I'm not sure if I should be the one to say it first. I don't know how she'd take it.

Since I'm at the apartment already I figure I might as well take a piss before heading on. Ashbee's is only six blocks down the way, across from the freeway entrance, and it really doesn't take that long to walk there. I'm sitting on the can when Biff calls again. Normally I wouldn't answer while on the toilet, but I know it'll just piss him off more if I don't answer.

"You weren't kidding about nine o'clock, huh?"

"I'm on my way, Biff."

"If you're over an hour late, it's a no-call no-show. I could write you up for this."

"I'm practically there," I say, and flush the toilet. I can hear Biff laughing on the other end but he won't give me the satisfaction of knowing I've broken his Boss Man exterior.

"Save it," he growls. "Ten minutes."

I'm there in twenty.

Biff isn't waiting at the side door like usual to let me in because it's after nine and we're already open. I go right through the automatic glass doors and walk across the sales floor. "Hey, Devin," Cherry calls to me from one of the bedroom displays where she's fluffing pillows.

"Hey, Cherry. I brought coffee!"

She follows me into the back room and snags a cup. "Thanks, kiddo." Cherry's only three years older than me which is why I guess she thinks calling me "kiddo" is funny. She goes back out onto the sales floor.

Biff comes out of his office into the break room. I hold the Styrofoam cup out to him like a shield. His big hand wraps around it and lifts it to his lips. He eyes me as he gulps down about half the cup.

"It's cold," he grunts, and sets the cup back on the table.

"That's it, I'm suing." I stamp my foot. "Serve me tepid coffee, will they? I *just* bought this."

"Clock in and get in here," he says, heading back into the tiny office. I punch my card and follow him. Biff Tipping is a big man, like a bear who transmogrified into a person. He moves uncertainly in his new, plastic environment, navigating around desks and chairs like he wishes he'd just stayed a frikkin' bear.

The orthopedic roller chair creaks under Biff's weight as he sits himself down in front of the old Mac. He scrolls through some Excel files and shows me how to do the payroll. He takes this shadowing thing quite literally; he expects me to stand behind him and watch while he goes through the motions, and not say anything. It's been this way for two weeks. Mostly I tune out and start thinking about things like Carmelle's boobs or a nice plate of seafood pasta, but I haven't had either of those things in a long time and it is getting hard to picture them.

"All right." Biff clicks off the computer and swivels around. "Get your vest on and get on the floor. We'll cover daily scheduling over your lunch break."

"Come on, Biff, you're gonna make me work through lunch?"

"No, Devin, you're making *me* work through lunch. Don't make me write this up."

He's not kidding, he really does take all this seriously. He's not even middle management yet, but I'm pretty sure that's as far as his ambition goes. Maybe someday he hopes to find a nice lady who isn't intimidated by his bear-like exterior (or a nice gentleman who wants to dress him in some leather chaps) and settle down in a double-wide trailer park a few blocks away, raise some kids or some alpacas, and retire with just enough money to get on food stamps. I guess my offering of cold coffee does not factor into his plans anywhere.

I give him a stiff salute. "Sir, yes sir." A hard turn on my heel and I am out the door before he can wield his smidgen of power again.

Out on the floor I take a sweep of the minimal activity. Ashbee's is inside a square building but its innards are circular, a feng shui sphere of maximum efficiency. A moat of various display rooms (living, dining, bed, kitchen) encircles a hub—or castle—of register computers where I see Cherry click-click-clicking away, drawing up a contract for the young couple standing near the Baroque ottomans. The most expensive stuff at Ashbee's is positioned nearest the entrance, fanning out into less desirable items, until finally hitting the clearance nexus—funky stains? mysterious odors? you want 'em, we got 'em!—behind the register hub. To be honest, I'm not so good at the hard sell, but I do all right on commissions simply by hovering around the clearance section, being extremely helpful.

Cutting between the nexus and the kids' mattresses is a hallway that leads to the customer bathrooms and our staff-only back room. Here we have a little kitchenette break room that connects to the manager's office and the loading dock. The office—Biff's cave—is unremarkable, except for the life-saving employee bathroom which the customers can't know we have, otherwise we'd appear cruel in their time of crisis ("Whaddya mean, the bathrooms are out of order?

Where do you go?"). The loading dock, on the other hand, is a remarkable example of poor planning as the doors leading to and from the dock aren't quite wide enough to fit a king-sized bed through. Most of our delivery guys understand this and will pull around to the front to drop off their loads, but whenever the regional manager comes around—a twig of a man who takes himself even more seriously than Biff—we have to fill the space with as much of the smaller furniture as possible so it doesn't look like we're wasting space. (The furniture we deliver to your home actually comes from a warehouse on the other side of town with adequately-sized doors.) Every dollar counts and everything is dollars. That's what the corporate sponge is constantly telling us, anyway.

Faintly, I hear the sound of a toilet flushing and a few seconds later Brad comes out, still zipping up his requisite beige khaki pants. Cherry has printed up her documents and is going over them with the couple, making them comfortable on a purple velvet love seat. I'm tapping my fingers on the register desk, rethinking my decision to skip breakfast.

Brad eyes Cherry with her customers and approaches me. "What the hell is she doing?"

"Good morning, Brad. I am well, thank you for asking. And yourself?"

"Did Cherry just sell them people a fucking couch?" He hooks his thumb in their general direction, his eyes bloodshot and screaming at me.

"Why, you want to congratulate her?"

"That's my fucking sale!"

Brad keeps his voice down when he swears, but he swears pretty much every other sentence. It's like Tourette's. Mostly customers ignore it, thinking it really is Tourette's, or it makes them feel like home. The only people I know of who he's ever offended with his colorful language are the higher ups—thus Brad is conveniently scheduled off when they make their bi-weekly visits—and Carmelle at last year's company picnic. To his credit, he was trying to be nice—well, his version of nice—but it came out like this: "Fuck, how you doing, Carmelle? Goddamn, your girlfriend's real sweet, a real fucking nut grabber on the floor, fucks 'em like dogs, fuck." He was trying to tease me about how little I actually sell, but Carmelle took it the wrong way and possessively whisked me away from him, and the entire picnic, in favor of going shoe shopping.

She said, "I don't know how you can put up with that dick."

I said, "He kind of reins it in at work."

Now, he is saying, "That whore cunt-grabber, I fucking told her, I told her, it's my goddamn turn, Devin, fuck."

There are always two or more salesfolk on the floor at a time. To keep commissions fair, we take turns on who gets to schmooze with the next customer through the door. No matter who it is. Sometimes you get stuck with the teens just stopping in to wander around on break from their fast-food gigs, but fair is fair.

Suddenly, in Brad's predicament, I see an opportunity to flex my fledgling shift-leader muscles. I look around the store for Biff, but he must still be in the office doing Big Boy stuff. I want him to observe how expertly I handle this squabble, so he can write *that* up, and almost consider paging him over the loud speaker, but that would seriously undercut my sincerity.

"Now, Bradley," I say, gracelessly dropping a hand on his slumped shoulder. "Calm down. Don't go jumping to conclusions before you have all the facts. I'm sure she just forgot the rotation schedule. Or maybe the customers approached her and she couldn't very well give them the cold shoulder and wait until you were done taking a shit or toking up, right?"

"I'm damn well gonna find out!" He starts toward them, but I hold him back and force him to look at me.

"You will do no such thing," I tell him, invoking the power of all mothers and elementary school teachers before me. "The sale is done. Look, they're walking away. You can get the next one."

"She should give me her fucking commission," Brad whines. "What if the next one's a dud?"

"I'll give her a warning," I say reassuringly. Brad looks at me like, *With what authority?* "I'll tell Biff about it," I amend. "I mean, I'll report it." Still getting used to the lower-middle-management lingo.

"If this shit happens again, Devin, I swear to fuck...."

But Brad doesn't have time to swear to fuck because a tiny mechanized bell bleats through the sound of the automatic doors whooshing open, and we turn our heads in unison to watch an octogenarian hobble in, sporting a tweed coat and corduroy pants and two wobbly canes. Brad slowly turns back around to look at me.

"I'm sorry." I cringe out an apology. It's clear this old dude is only here to escape the heat of the morning or possibly to curl up in a nice soft bed to die alone, like cats do.

We watch him shuffle at a snail's crawl to ease himself down into the nearest deluxe leather recliner. Finally, Brad sighs, mutters something about crotch lickers under his breath, and heads over to the man's side.

Cherry comes back over to the hub and starts filing away the paperwork from her sale. "What a pleasant couple," she beams. "They're having a baby and they're completely remodeling the guest room for her. They bought the complete Shirley Temple bedroom set, mattress frills and everything."

"You stole Brad's sale," I tell her.

"Oh, he'll get over it. He was in the bathroom, for crying out loud. This will teach him to hold it next time."

"That's not the point, Cherry."

"Like hell. Look, Devin, if you're bleeding so bad for the guy, why don't you give up your turn for him?"

That isn't the point either, but it does sound like a workable idea. "Brilliant, Cherry. I will do that." I remember my newly acquired leadership role and add, "And hopefully you will learn from my upstanding example."

Cherry laughs. "You just hate customers."

"I don't hate customers."

"Sure you do. That's why you want to work your way up to management, so you can hide in the back room all day and masturbate, like Biff."

"Okay, A, Biff is probably not masturbating. And B, you may have a point. But I don't hate customers, I'm just shy around them."

"Well, sister, if that's all it is, I can get you over that."

"Can you?"

"Sure. It's a little trick I use to put myself at ease with each and every customer, to remind myself that I have all the power in this dynamic." Cherry leans in conspiratorially close to my ear and whispers, "I simply picture them all with cocks in their mouths."

I'm stunned into silence. Cherry widens her eyes and smiles at me expectantly.

"Cocks?" I ask.

She nods. "In their mouth." Her smile broadens.

"Even the old people?"

"*Especially* the old people. It's a whole mind-over-matter thing. People use the same technique to get over their fear of public speaking."

"I'm pretty sure those people just picture the crowd in their underwear."

Cherry waves her hand through the air, dismissing the idea. "Please. How pussy is that?"

"I don't think I want to envision any cocks in any mouths today."

"Oh, come on, just because you're this huge gaymo doesn't mean this technique can't work for you, too."

"Cherry...."

"I'm sorry, huge lezmo."

"I don't think it will work for me."

"You never know until you try it, right? Here, someone's coming in right now, try it on her. I got your back!"

"Cherry!" I try to protest but she's unnaturally strong for a girl of such slight frame. She drags me around the desks and pushes me out of the hub. I bang my knee on the corner of a glass coffee table and look up to make sure the customer didn't notice.

As I near her, something about the woman seems familiar. Maybe it's the way she is standing, kind of carelessly, shoulders humped, arms held close to the chest, knees bent, head angled to one side, inspecting the oak end tables near the door. Maybe it's the clothes she's wearing, combat boots, navy camo pants at least one size too big for her small frame, and over that, draping to just above the knee, a white spaghetti-strapped sundress flecked with small, light blue flowers. I'm pretty much on top of her now and I can see her white bra straps underneath her dress straps. Her lengthy dark brown hair moves over her deeply tanned bare shoulder, indicating she has turned her head and is now staring directly at me.

"Can I help you?" That's my line, but she says it to me. This close, she almost smells familiar, like sweat and popcorn, but not in a gross way. Kind of alluring, actually.

That's when I tear my eyes away from her bra and look at her face. She smirks, kind of her signature bad-ass smirk, and takes off her oversized sunglasses to stare me down with those big, brown eyes.

"Should I repeat the question?" asks Renni Ramirez. Renni Fucking Ramirez.

Here in rural Ohio, we might be behind the times in many areas as far as the wider world is concerned (the height of fashion still largely involves denim), but we do have a second-run movie theater in the strip mall, and some of us can afford cable. I have personally seen *Rising Evil* twelve times, mainly to educate my friends about the lesbian subtext totally happening between Ms. Ramirez and her co-star Ms. Zhirenkov, but also for the hundred and twenty minutes of gore-splattering zombie killing. I'd know those sexy-angry eyes anywhere, that resonant rasp of a voice, those well-toned arms normally exposed by a form-fitting man's sleeveless undershirt (personally, I'm a fan of the sundress). You might think the three-hundred-foot movie screen version of Renni Ramirez would be more intimidating than the tiny five-foot-six version two feet away, but you would be wrong.

The only thing that saves me from complete and utter paralysis is remembering, however involuntarily, Cherry's perverse advice. Suddenly I'm no longer stunned to silence by Renni's gorgeous, unreal face, because the giant penis floating beside her head distracts me. I don't know why it's so giant, maybe to reflect how ridiculous I think this visualization technique is. Thankfully, the penis (flaccid, for some reason) does not get anywhere close to Renni's mouth; it hovers impotently behind her, until, slowly, as I come back to myself, it fades into the arm of an antique rocking chair.

"I'm sorry, no. What? I'm sorry." Well, so much for playing it cool.

But Renni Ramirez just laughs, a Sunday morning laugh, casual and unhurried. "Don't sweat it."

This is when I realize if I can sell her some type of furniture, or even just one of the lamps that are technically display-only, she will have to sign a contract and then I can have her autograph without having to stoop to some generic fangirl level and ask her for one. Genius! Carmelle would flip out, hug me, maybe kiss me, maybe more. One of our first dates was a cook-in movie fest where I made her dinner and we watched the fourth movie in the *Shut Up and Drive* series, or at least the first fifteen minutes before Renni Ramirez's character was unceremoniously killed off. We consoled ourselves over this injustice by fucking heartily for several hours.

"So you came all this way to buy a couch, huh?" I'm trying to take her cue and play it nonchalant, but my pits are sweating and the penis is starting to reform.

"Right," she laughs again. "You guys deliver to L.A., right?"

I laugh, a little bit too long because her eyes start to meander a little to the left of my head, and I wonder what floating appendage she might be envisioning.

"Well, if you really are looking for something, I could help you, or...."

"You're sweet," she says, clipping her sunglasses to the bosom of her dress. "What's your name?"

I point out my name tag, conveniently close to my nipple, which is slightly visible beneath my requisite blue vest and white shirt. "Devin."

"Ah, I played a chick with that name a long time ago."

"Yeah." *I know! It was your tough-as-nails, "First day on the job and I gotta deal with fucking zombies?", take-no-shit rookie cop in* Rising Evil. *I've seen that movie twelve times and I've made everyone I know and love watch it because I cannot truly love anyone who hasn't seen that movie because you rocked so hard in it rocks are ashamed they can't rock as hard as you and who the hell's decision was it to kill off your character because I just like to pretend she survived and ran away with Jennifer Zhirenkov's character and they saved the world together which sounds like some kind of fanfiction 'shipping thing but I don't write that shit, I promise.* "That movie was cool."

"Devin, you're the first person to recognize me all weekend."

"Oh. I'm sorry."

She laughs again, throwing her whole head into it and punching my shoulder like a pal. "It's nice! I was starting to think I didn't rate in...."

She struggles to recall the name of our quiet oasis, and I fill the blank for her: "Buttfuck, Ohio?"

Somehow I knew she would appreciate this. She laughs enthusiastically, and I laugh too, and she says, "Shit," like I just said the best thing in the world and she can't believe it.

I can't believe it. I'm building a rapport with Renni Fucking

Ramirez. I desperately want to text Carmelle and tell her all about it, but whipping out the cell phone right now would definitely kill the moment. I'm already reconstructing our encounter for story-time later: *And then I said....*

I feel a presence at my shoulder before the smell of damp socks and toffee hard candy assaults me. I turn to see the old man Brad had been busy with a few minutes ago, shuffling excitedly by me. He kind of nudges my shoulder a bit with his tweed arm, the stitching scratching my skin, as he ambles forward on his dual canes.

"Excuse me," he says to Renni Ramirez. "Are you America Ferrera?"

There's a beat in which Renni Ramirez's response to this query is unpredictable. She kind of cocks her head to eyeball the old man, the shadow of a smile still gracing her lips, one hand on her hip, the other absentmindedly fiddling with a fold in her dress. Then she sweeps her eyes back in my direction, and I know this is my moment, this is when I get to decide both our fates, maybe even the fate of the old man. Whatever gesture I make now, whatever words I let fall out of my mouth, however minutely expressed, however softly whispered, will set the tone for Renni Ramirez's response. Glib, I think, how do I project glibness?

Finally, I take a page from all the stoners who ever tried to convince my high school English teacher that they were paying attention to his lecture on *Lord of the Flies*. I close my eyes to half-slits, cross my arms over my chest, and nod once, slowly.

Renni Ramirez sweeps her eyes back to the eagerly patient old man. "Yep," she says. "That's me."

"Oh goodness but you're taller in real life, and well fit," the old man exclaims.

"It's for a movie I'm doing," she explains. "*A Midsummer Night's Furniture Store*. It's a re-imagining."

"That's excellent!" The old man and I are actually thinking the exact same thing but for entirely different reasons. Renni's smirk takes up permanent residence on her face as the old man continues speaking. "My nieces just love your show, *Ugly Confetti,* they talk about it all the time when I visit. You wear glasses in that, though. They showed me an episode or two. I didn't really get it, but they love it. I watch

*M*A*S*H* myself, sometimes the news. I usually can't sit still for that long. Can I have your autograph? For my nieces."

"Sure, papa," she says, making me wish absurdly that I was "papa." "Got a pen?"

"Not on my person as such," he says, patting down his coat, then his slacks. "I have one in my Firebird. Let me just run and get it."

Running, of course, is a relative term. We watch him scoot towards the double glass automatic doors, standing shoulder to shoulder, a hair's breadth away from touching. When the glass doors slide open, he is taken aback and nearly tilts over, but rights himself and continues on his way.

"That man has a Firebird?" Renni says under her breath.

"That, or dementia," I say, and Renni snorts a little air out through her nose in a way that makes me pee myself a little.

And that is when it happens. There in the soft haze of this perfectly surreal moment between myself and someone whose image I have repeatedly masturbated to, materializes my first ever real-life zombie.

It's the same guy from the coffee shop earlier in the morning, who I had assumed was just some harmless drunk trying to start his day right. Now as he hobbles along the sidewalk, perpendicular to the sluggish trajectory of the old man who just left the store, seconds away from contact, I can clearly see something is far more wrong with him. His gait has become even more broken, his arms dragging along at his sides. Though one of his ankles is twisted at a very painful-looking angle, he pushes it forward, scraping it along the pavement. From his dangling hands drips a dark, slick substance that I don't think is coffee. And his face. Fuck, his face. The skin droops down as if melting, turned some sort of greenish-yellow hue that has nothing to do with sun exposure, and his scalp is peeling worse than ever, whole chunks of dirty hair displaced, revealing the dry sores. The same non-coffee substance leaks from his mouth, splattering his befouled shirt and torn jeans.

Renni Ramirez grips my wrist instinctively and clenches hard as the old man cuts off the drunk man, who I now think is injured or an escaped mental patient or....

"Maybe he needs help," I say.

"You don't want to go out there," Renni says.

The doors slide shut on her words, and on the howling scream of the old man as the drunk guy, who I'm now certain is a zombie, lurches forward with unfathomable speed and bites off the old man's cheek.

For a second, perhaps two, we both just stand there, her fingernails digging into the underside of my wrist, my bladder threatening to spill, my eyes unable to look away from whatever the hell is happening outside. I know what is happening outside. One man is ripping apart another man. Except he can't be a man, I know through some place deep and buried, leftover from Man's prehistoric hunting days, some natural survival instinct, that the attacker is something far more dangerous than a man. And because I've watched so many movies in this piece-of-shit, do-nothing town, and because I don't believe in God or divine invention, and because I've read about the fucked-up experiments science has sanctioned in its quest for knowledge since the invention of psychoanalysis, I know this man is a fucking zombie.

The old man out there, literally caught in the zombie's jaws, has no hope of survival. But all of us in here—Renni Ramirez, Cherry, Brad and Biff—we can still make it through this. There is still time to run. But only if the zombie doesn't see us first.

I whip around, tearing my arm away from Renni's death grip. "Cherry!" I shout. I spot her and Brad in the hub, emphatically gesturing at each other behind the registers. They didn't hear the old man's screams, but they see now, looking beyond me, the violence reaching a crescendo outside. "Cherry, hit the lights! Turn off the fucking lights!"

"What the fuck?" Brad's jaw drops and he starts toward the door, but Cherry is a smart lady; she grabs Brad by the shoulder and twists him around, marching him toward the light switches on the wall near the Serta Sleepers.

"Everybody hide!" I shout.

"Lock the door, lock the fucking door," Renni calmly suggests. She's clutching her sunglasses like they're my wrist.

"I can't," I tell her, "they're automatic. Locking them requires a key. Biff keeps it...."

Thwack! We both jump back at the sound of flesh slamming against the double doors. It's the old man's upper thigh, sheathed in blood, inching its way down the glass, streaking a crimson stain in its wake. I can't really see through the blood splatter, but I can see enough movement to know the zombie is still going to town. The old man's dismembered thigh slides to the ground, and when it hits the outside mat it triggers the automatic sensor and the doors swish open.

The zombie looks up.

I don't look at him long enough to know if his eyes, surely lacking in retinal reception by this stage in his zombification, got a chance to register my presence. I grab Renni Ramirez's elbow without thinking and shove her along the circle until we can dip behind a large black leather sofa. Cherry and Brad didn't make it to the lights, but I see them ducked behind the register desks, Cherry's manicured finger over Brad's scowling lips. I hear my heart beating in my chest, and become aware that I can feel Renni's heart beating against my left arm.

I dare not peek out to see what the zombie is up to, but I don't hear him enter. The doors will stay open for as long as the thigh remains on the sensor, which means either the zombie will reclaim his meal, find a tastier morsel somewhere else in the plaza, or come exploring.

Over Renni's hot breathing in my ear, I hear the distinct scraping of a twisted foot along the concrete. He's coming in.

Chapter 2

Eat You? I Hardly Know You

I'm crouched here behind this overturned table, trying to stop the bleeding from my calf, and the words I kept myself from saying to Carmelle scream out through my rapidly thinning blood. Maybe if I said it more—or at all—she wouldn't sleep on her side every night with her back to me, uninviting. That one morning when she woke up early, careful not to wake me, and stole into the kitchen to make blueberry pancakes and chocolate chip waffles and fruit salad and smoothies, and she woke me up anyway because we live in a studio apartment, and I was irritated until I smelled what she was cooking and then I felt too guilty to eat any of it and then she got angry and left for the day and I had to clean everything up, which was irritating—that morning, I should have woken up and just said it. I'm the one who asked her to move in with me on our one year anniversary when I tried so hard to think of something special to plan but my car had broken down earlier in the week and I didn't get that raise I'd been counting on and my gerbil died and even though I'd sent that check to the electric company weeks ago when I had the money in my account the company didn't cash it in until that week when I had thirty-five dollars to my name and so it bounced and I never had to deal with that before so I was freaking out. When it came time to take Carmelle out, I showed up to her dorm room on my own two feet, looked at her with the saddest eyes I've ever looked at anyone, held a copy of my key out to her, and just said, "Please." So maybe she has lived with me all these months out of pity, and she's stopped having sex with me because the allure of sleeping with someone dangerously close to bankruptcy just doesn't get her up anymore, and if I'd just say it, just suck it up and say it, without thinking about it, without questioning, just fucking say it.... Maybe then she'd say it back. But my leg won't stop bleeding, I'm trapped here watching the red run into my sock, filling my shoe, which tightens as my foot swells.

How did I ever let that God forsaken zombie get close enough to take a chunk outta me?

After that zombie comes scraping into the store, his limp steps dragging over the sensor in the floor that causes the mechanical buzzer above the automatic doors to announce his presence—*dong!*—everything happens so slowly, just slowly enough to feel unreal, almost slowly enough to feel escapable. The sound of Renni's heart slamming inside her chest next to me, her hot breath against my neck as we both strain to keep still and quiet, is louder than the scraping zombie mere feet away from us, who almost doesn't even exist but for an intermittent suck-swallow sound that I assume he makes with his mouth (neither of us pokes our heads out to sneak a peek from behind our leather and wood shield). Since the fluorescent lights still burn bright above us, the zombie casts no shadow as he ambles about; the only way I can triangulate his position is by trying to hear his scraping, his sucking, and by stealing glances at Cherry and Brad, who are just visible at this angle, crouched low behind a register desk. If the zombie circles around this side of the loop, they'll have to duck back, but for now they have a better bead on the thing's location, and instinctively Cherry communicates this knowledge back to me by mouthing single words. "Post," meaning he is near the load-bearing column by the front door that marks the start of our mahogany end-table collection; "Water," meaning he has reached the water beds; "Coffee," meaning he has wandered back into the inner circle of the tiled moat near the coffee tables, like the one I bumped into only minutes ago, trying to get to my new customer, who is now my partner in hiding.

The wind picks up outside and blows a chill into the store, and an odor: coppery and sour, the smell of the old man's moldering thigh. From the parking lot I think I can hear sounds of motors turning over or turning off, car doors slamming, maybe a person screaming, maybe a siren wailing. Maybe someone out doing their early morning Sunday shopping before church has seen the aftermath of the carnage, or witnessed the attack themselves, and has called the police. I briefly considered this tack myself, but the second I moved my hand to dig into my khaki pants pocket for my cell phone, the zombie's scraping stopped and that sucking sound started. I'm afraid he can hear the faint whispers of my fingers brushing against the fabric of my pants, maybe he can even hear the muscles or tendons flexing underneath my skin, or the joints creaking in my body, and he stops to suck at the air, like a snake, trying to sense what direction these impossibly soft sounds are coming from. So I've stayed still, kept my ears open, my eyes on Cherry, the backs of my knuckles resting slightly against Renni's knee, and am hoping something happens soon to resolve this thing—the police show up, someone outside makes enough noise to distract the zombie into a chase, the zombie gets bored and leaves, something.

When something finally does happen, I'm reminded of that little nugget of condescension masquerading as wisdom espoused by parents across the nation: "Be careful what you wish for."

From the back room comes the sound of the toilet flushing. The zombie's scraping feet pause, and the air *slick-slooks* out of or around or into him. My body tenses up as my mind screams, "No!" I know Renni is thinking something similar because she clasps the back of my t-shirt near the belt of my pants. Over in the hub, Cherry and Brad exchange an anguished look, and then Cherry turns to me and mouths, "Biff!"

The latch of the back room door clicks and the hinges squeak as it opens. Almost immediately upon entering the floor, Biff is speaking loudly, slapping his hands together like *mush, mush*. "All right, kids, we got an unexpected delivery of slightly irregular recliners out back. The delivery guys are new, didn't know to come around front, and are now refusing to budge, so we gotta work with them. Come on, guys, let's— Cherry? Brad? Something fascinating to you two behind that desk I should know about?"

He'd been walking toward the hub as he spoke, so that Cherry and Brad's position had been obscured by another register desk, but now they are exposed. I can see Biff now too, tail of his button-up cauliflower-blue shirt—assistant manager's special—flapping against his butt where he'd failed to tuck it in all the way; small square of moist toilet paper clinging to the heel of his Payless black work boots. From their hiding place, Brad and Cherry frantically wave at Biff, mouthing the word "Run!" so urgently it almost comes out as a hiss. I still can't see the zombie, but a low, wet rattle swells from his general direction, until it becomes a deep moan.

"What is going on here, you two?" Biff demands. "Where is Devin? What— Oh my God!" Biff's face registers shock, but not fear, as he finally spots the zombie. I rock forward on the balls of my feet, preparing to spring into action, expecting the zombie to launch its attack, but the zombie doesn't move, and Renni's hand steadies me.

But Biff does move. He makes the same mistake I almost made earlier, but being Biff, he actually follows through. "Oh my God, sir—" he steps toward the zombie, arms out, seeking to comfort, to help. "Are you hurt? What happened? Let me help you."

And this part moves slower than all the others. Biff's right leg bends and lifts into one final step; the zombie crinkles into view on his broken legs. His arms rise up, calling to Biff, and then I rise up, literally calling to Biff by screaming his name with my mouth and workable larynx. Biff's eyes shift over to meet mine, flashing some kind of emotion I don't have time to read before the zombie, through some bizarre surge of strength and speed, lurches forward and attaches his jaw to Biff's neck. I hear the crunch of skin and bone breaking together, like the sound of a thousand competitive eaters chowing down on a swimming pool-sized bucket of fried chicken wings. I watch the blood spurt from him like a malfunctioning fountain, and Biff's face contorts in a way no face should contort. His body goes slack, and the zombie lowers him to the floor with surprising gentleness, like a lover.

My focus zooms out from this action to take in Brad and Cherry, who have leaped out of hiding. Brad's stringing obscenities together to form some new language even a Yale linguistics professor wouldn't be able to decipher; Cherry's mascara streaks down her face with her tears, her mouth alternately sucking in and spitting out the dripping makeup through gasps as she screams.

And Biff on the floor, silent under the zombie's deafening mastication.

The only other sound I hear before my own scream and pounding of shoes on linoleum tile is Renni's urgent whisper, "Don't." But I do. I run toward Biff's prone body, and kick the zombie in the ribs.

His flesh is softer than I'm expecting, giving easily beneath the force of my kick so that I can feel his insides sliding around on the arch of my foot. The zombie makes no sound, but he rolls off of Biff, and I grab at Biff's shoulders. They're too slick with his own blood for me to get a good grip.

"Come on, Biff," I hear myself shout at him. "Come on! You're a bear, goddammit! Biff, you're a bear, get up!"

I guess, looking back, that's when the stupidity took over. Or it may have been this: Renni Ramirez shouts into my ear, "Devin, stop," grabs at my flailing arms, and I—caught up in the desperation of the moment, lost in the pale emptiness of Biff's half-closed eyes and swimming in his blood—I elbow Renni Ramirez in the face.

Her blood stains the dry skin of my elbow, warm and sticky. She stumbles back, my eyes register—before my brain fully comprehends—what I've done. I start, "I'm—" thinking to apologize, and that's when the zombie takes me down.

He slams into me like an overzealous linebacker who's finally seeing Astroturf after twenty straight games on the bench, wrapping his arms around my shoulders so that my own arms are pinned to my side, and pitching me onto the floor beside Biff's expanding pool of blood. The zombie's stench overwhelms me, the hot wet garbage stink of the homeless mixed with the coppery sweetness of Biff's blood and vital organs, a piece of which dangles out of the zombie's drooping mouth as he looms over me. He moans from deep inside his throat, his own personal brand of salivating now that his glands have stopped working. Now I can see—and hear—that the slick suck-swallow sound wasn't emanating from a smacking of lips or tongue, but from a hole the size of my fist in his neck, exposing black and dark crimson tendons and other tissues, fresh blood running into it, something inside moving up and down, up and down, in time with the sucking sound—as if this zombie were breathing. Impossible.

But I can't get caught up in the mechanics for too long because the zombie has picked out some tasty real estate along the shore of my carotid artery and is about to make a down payment. I'm thrashing, and he's inches away from closing escrow, when the blue porcelain lamp shatters against his crusty forehead.

The impact halts him but he doesn't move as the shards rain down around him and onto my face. I tilt my head back and look to see Cherry, scooping up lamps from side tables in the bedroom displays. She chucks them at the zombie, mostly missing, lamps exploding like tiny pipe bombs all around us. Brad holds the back-room door open, desperately calling for everyone to move their fucking asses and run already.

The zombie might not be moving, but he is distracted. I knee him in the crotch once, feel the improbable give there, and remember what I'm dealing with. I shove the thumbs of both my hands into his eyes and push until they pop and ooze—disgustingly easy—and I'm touching socket, or maybe brains. The zombie falls back long enough for me to crab-scramble out from under him, and then Renni Ramirez is lifting me from under my armpits into a standing position.

"I'm sorry," I say.

She sucks blood and air in through her already bruising nose and says, "Make it up to me later."

From behind us, Cherry shouts, "You guys, run over here!" She tosses one more lamp in our general direction before spinning on her heel and darting over to Brad at the open back-room doorway.

And that's when it happens. Fifteen feet from safety, my hand swallowed by the warm and nimble fingers of Renni Ramirez's hand as she leads me away from the still-fresh tragedy. I feel the individual points of the zombie's teeth puncture my calf like stings from a swarm of bees. I kick back without looking behind me, without even stopping in my sprint, feel his rotting face give out under my heel, his teeth bursting from his mouth, his moan muffled. I'm in the break room, door slammed shut behind me, before I register any pain.

"Out of the way!" Brad waves us away from the lockless door, overturns the plastic break room table in one clunky move, and lift-drags it in place in front of the door.

"Brad!" Cherry shouts at him, not yet able to lower her voice to match the calm and quiet of the break room. "Bradley, stop!"

A *thud* crashes against the door, causing Cherry to yelp and the rest of us to jump. Another thud follows, then another.

"Quick." Brad starts pointing at anything movable in the room—the chairs, the microwave, the mini fridge, the dish rack. "Help me move this fucking stuff, for shit's sake, that thing's trying to get in."

"Bradley, no," Cherry restarts her protest.

"Cherry, what the fuck kind of death wish you got? Fuck." Brad rips the microwave from the wall and stacks it at the bottom of the door, against the table, then goes back for the chairs.

"But, Brad—"

"But your ass, Cherry, grab a fucking chair."

"—It opens out! The door opens *out*!"

Brad stops, one folding chair clutched under each arm. The thudding against the door continues at a predictable clip as the zombie, now blind, repeatedly throws its body into it.

Brad says, "Shit," and lets the chairs clatter to the floor. Cherry covers her face with her hands and starts crying loudly.

I raise my hand like I'm back in Sunday school, but I don't wait for anyone to call on me. "Um, guys? Could someone get me the first aid kit, maybe?"

All eyes turn to me, and I figure this is as good a time as any to collapse against the wall, so I do. Instantly, Renni's arms are around me, easing me to the ground, which only reminds me of how gently—how tenderly—the zombie lowered Biff to the ground. Tears sting my eyes, and I try to tell myself they are only there because the pain in my calf has finally caught up with my brain, and it hurts worse than passing kidney stones, which was the worst pain I'd ever experienced up until now.

"I broke my arm in three places when I was thirteen," Renni Ramirez tells me as she maneuvers my upper body to slip off my blue Ashbee's vest. "That was my worst pain. At least I remember it as the worst."

I hadn't realized I'd said the thing about the kidney stones out loud. My head feels hot, heavy, and sweat has begun to seep from my brow. Renni wipes it away with the back of her hand. Then Cherry hands her a fifth of Kentucky's Best Bourbon.

"For me?" I ask, smacking my lips.

Renni laughs in that way of hers and I almost forget about my leg injury. She uncaps the bottle, scrunches up my vest in her hand, and pours the whiskey over it. "Sanitizing," she says. "Saw it in a movie once," and she winks at me.

Brad comes back into view, kneeling down beside Cherry, and sets the first aid kit by my knee. I personally know that thing hasn't been replenished since 1983, so that all it contains at this point is an ice pack, a box of circular band-aids, a tube of Neosporin, and maybe some Advil. Which, truthfully, I wouldn't sneeze at right now.

"Hope you didn't love these," Renni says. She tears my blood-soaked khakis along the seam, starting at the ankle and stopping at the knee. She uses the drier part of one of the flaps to wipe the blood around the wound, and then, without warning, she pours some bourbon on it. It stings too much for me to even cry out. I close my eyes and bite my lip and pee a little but hopefully nobody notices.

When I open my eyes again, Renni is stuffing the wound with the alcohol soaked rag, and wrapping an ACE bandage around my leg and the rag, pinning it closed once it's all wrapped up. I guess Biff did do a refill, after all.

"Brad, right?" Renni addresses him. She bites down on an individual packet of Advil and tears the foil open with her teeth. "Get her some water?"

This is when Brad finally realizes that the woman giving him instructions is Renni Fucking Ramirez. I can see it in his face, which goes slack in surprise, and then tightens back up in disbelief. But he doesn't say anything. He gets to his feet and seconds later I hear the faucet running.

"Oh, that makes sense," Cherry says, in a distant kind of way I've never heard from her before. Her mascara has created a river of makeup down her face, and as her tears dry, the river cakes into dirty clumps. Maybe it's the fever, but her look is crazed, her eyes wide, pupils dilated, irises vibrating. She's looking at Renni, trembling fingers pressed to her lips. "It's all a dream." She laughs a little, a hummingbird trill. "Of course. That same dream I always have about coming to work naked, meeting Renni Ramirez, and watching a zombie attack my friends. Yeah."

"It's not a cock-licking dream, Cherry," Brad says sweetly as he holds the cup of water out to me. Outside, the zombie continues its thud-thud-thudding assault on the defenseless door.

"You're not naked," Renni says, pointing out the flaw in Cherry's dream logic. I can't hear well enough to know if she sounds disappointed about this.

"Oh. Right," Cherry concedes.

"Here, swallow these." Renni drops two Advil caplets on my tongue and tilts the cup of water against my lips. Before the water enters my mouth, I have a split second to taste the remnants of Renni Ramirez's hands on the chalky pills on my tongue. They taste like she smells—a spiced musk, like a fresh-baked specialty bread only served on Sundays.

I swallow the pills. The zombie thuds. I think about Carmelle. Brad says, "I'm calling the police."

Cherry knocks Brad's cell phone out of his hands. "You can't! There's a zombie out there! The police aren't equipped to handle a zombie."

"Goddammit motherfucking Devin needs a fucking doctor, Cherry."

"So we'll take her. It'll be faster than waiting for an ambulance anyway. It's just off the second highway exit."

"Zombie's blind, anyway," Renni reminds everyone. Lightly, she pats my bandaged leg. "Pretty pathetic to let that thing bite on you now."

"What if there are more of them?" Cherry says, working herself up. "Have you ever heard of one single zombie traveling alone?"

"I don't know what the fuck was wrong with that shit-swallowing hole out there," Brad says, getting up to look for his phone. "But he wasn't no fucking zombie."

Cherry gets up to follow him and debate with him on this point. I straighten up and lean over to grab the first aid kit. I find the ice pack, break it over my knee, and hand it to Renni.

"It really doesn't look too bad," I tell her, and I'm being honest. I mean, the nose is clearly broken, but the bruises and the swelling, even the blood, just deepen that mean-sexy look she's known for. Her smile kind of throws it off a bit, but I don't mind.

She holds the ice pack to her nose. "I can get you to the hospital," she says. "I'm parked out front."

"No!" Cherry overhears Renni. "No one else is risking going near that thing, whatever he is. He's already killed two people. We'll go out the loading dock. There's a delivery truck there, remember? We'll have them take us to the hospital."

I do vaguely remember Biff saying something like that before.... Well. I nod at Cherry. "Solid plan."

Renni puts her hands under my armpits again and lifts me up. I kind of wish she would stop doing that because I've been sweating so much since the attacks started, I must stink really badly under there, not to mention how damp it must feel, and now that stink and that dampness is getting all over her hands, but Renni doesn't seem to mind. I lean against her, testing weight out on my injured leg.

"We'll scout ahead," Brad offers. He and Cherry disappear out the door that leads to the loading dock, closing it behind them.

The steady rhythm of the thudding zombie keeps Renni Ramirez and me company as we wait for them to return.

I don't really want to say this next thing, because I'm afraid she'll take me up on the idea, but I feel strangely obligated to remind her. "You don't have to stay with us, you know."

"So you can blog about how big of a prick I am for bailing on you?" She gives my shoulder a quick squeeze. "Not a chance."

"You're not how I imagined you." It's not the first stupid thing I've said to Renni Ramirez, but it certainly is the latest.

"You've *imagined* me, have you?" She looks at me askance and arches a single eyebrow at me. I might as well have used the word "fantasized."

The best I can hope for is that my rising fever hides my blooming blush. "Well, I mean, um. My girlfriend's really into your movies."

Just then, Brad and Cherry come scrambling back into the break room, breathing hard and—if it's even possible—looking more ashen. Brad immediately drags the table from its ineffective position at the break room door to in front of the loading dock door. Since this door opens in, he gets no argument from Cherry.

After a moment, Cherry collects herself enough to explain: "I was right. There are more of them."

Brad expands, "Motherfucking beasts got one of them poor bastard drivers, other driver fucking took off, about shit his balls, man, fuck."

"They're swarming over the parking lot out there," Cherry continues. "Some of them are real...real *fresh*. They almost trick you into believing they're human, until they get close and you can see their eyes...." She shudders.

Brad stops piling things in front of the door long enough to wrap an arm around Cherry. She buries her head in his shoulder, and he strokes her sweat-tinged hair, softly cooing platitudes curiously devoid of obscenities.

"Okay," Renni says. "You two stay here."

"What?" Brad says. He and Cherry look at her.

"We're going. I'll send back help."

With that, she grabs my left wrist and drapes my arm over her shoulder, holding me by the waist with her other arm, so I can lean most of my weight on her, and she walks us to the break room door. She studies it for a couple of seconds, ignoring the sobbing protests of Cherry and mumbled arguments of Brad. I feel her body tense against mine, every muscle going rigid with anticipation. She pulls her right knee up to her chest, bares her teeth like a tigress defending her cubs, and releases her leg into the door with all the power of a raging bull. The jamb splinters the door frame as the door swings back, knocking with a bone-vibrating *crunch* into the blind zombie, who stumbles back into the opposite wall on impact. The door bounces off the zombie's destroyed face and swings back toward us. Renni elbows us over the threshold.

In the hall, maybe a foot from the zombie, we can hear its death rattle-cum-zombie-moan gearing up for an encore in the back of its throat. Black gunk seeps out of its eye holes and spills from its perpetually open mouth. If possible in the last ten minutes the thing has decayed even further, unless I just never noticed its corpse-gray skin, some kind of mucus leaking out of the pores on its outstretched arms.

Outstretched arms. The zombie is coming in for another attack.

Renni Ramirez has had enough of this zombie's shit.

As we pass by its leaking form, without even breaking stride, Renni lets go of my left arm, squeezes me a little tighter around the waist with her right arm, and lets loose her left arm like a force to be reckoned with. Her left hook connects with the zombie's loose jaw, sending its remaining teeth up into its skull with a sound like Gallagher sledgehammering an unsuspecting watermelon. Immediately, the rattle-moan cuts off, and the zombie falls to the ground like the pile of inert bones it was always meant to be.

Continuing toward the front of the store, Renni calls over her shoulder to Cherry and Brad in the break room, "Get out here and lock these fucking doors."

I try not to look at Biff's body as we step over him. At the automatic glass doors, our feet trample over the sensor that *dongs* our position. Renni pauses just long enough to kick the masticated thigh of the old man—already attracting enormous flies—out of the way. The glass doors slide closed behind us. I crane my head around to look over Renni's shoulder, and watch through the glass as the blurred images of Cherry and Brad use Biff's key to lock the doors. Cherry splays her palm on the glass and mouths, "Good luck." I nod back at her.

Renni whispers something that the wind whips away from me.

"What was that?" I ask loudly.

Somewhere to my right, the familiar death rattle begins to swell, quickly followed by a rising moan to my left. I look around quickly and it doesn't take me long to assess the situation: we're boned.

All across the parking lot, from behind beat-up Pintos, wood-paneled station wagons, twenty-foot pick-up trucks, and sensible sedans, come the zombies. Some crawl, missing parts of themselves, others drag their loose parts behind them, while still others, the healthy ones—the fresh ones, as Cherry called them—appear from around the side of the building, their footing terrifyingly sure. There are women, men, young and old; I don't have a lot of time to scrutinize their faces beyond their dead and empty eyes, but I would not be surprised to find I know some of them.

Without stopping, and through pinched-tight lips, Renni says, "I said, we can make it. As long as we're quiet."

Chapter 3

THE WEATHER IS HERE, WISH YOU WERE DEAD

ME AND CARMELLE HAVE LIVED IN THIS CRAPPY STUDIO apartment for about four months now. (In fact, I think the rent is due on Tuesday. Maybe my landlord is a zombie now, or a corpse, and I won't have to deal with it this month. Upside!) She'd been to my place many times before she accepted my key, but I don't think she realized how small it was until the night she moved in. She had a U-haul full of furniture that just wasn't gonna make it, but we compromised and swapped out some of my stuff for hers. For example, in exchange for her Papasan chair, I gave up the futon I'd salvaged from Ashbee's recycling program (it was only slightly stained, had three perfectly good legs, and the odor really wasn't that bad once you got used to it, though I did find myself waking up with a hankering for SpaghettiOs with hotdog meat most mornings); she gave up her vanity mirror to let me keep my vintage *90210* locker replica (she used it to hang up her dresses; before that, I'd been using it as a place to store my comic books). We had to go to Ashbee's for a new bed because the futon had been it, and there we squabbled not over prices but how much room we could afford to spare.

"If we get the king size, we'll have two inches of side space each," I told her.

"We can press it up against that one corner," she countered.

"Then you'll always have to climb over me to get to the bathroom."

"No, you'll always have to climb over me. I sleep on the right side."

"You've always slept on the left side."

"That was out of courtesy when I was staying over at *your* place. Now it's *my* place, too. I sleep on the right."

I wouldn't really call it bickering, more like playful ribbing, until one of us caved (me) and we got a double bed, the ancient Victorian kind with four posts and a thin veil thing that wraps around, for privacy. It's the fanciest thing we own and it looks ridiculous. Even with my discount, I'm still paying off my half. Anyway, the rest of our stuff went to storage until we can save up for a new place, which is a long way off if Carmelle keeps buying things like this: a thirty-seven-inch flat-screen TV. It's nice because we can mount it on the wall and sit on the bed to watch movies together, which we did a lot before she stopped being too interested in touching me. I was kind of annoyed at the extravagance of it until Carmelle came home one day with an Xbox 360 and my world was changed.

First person shooters. That's where it's at. I used nine sick days in the first two weeks we had that thing, going head to head with Carmelle or some friends when she wasn't around. There were western shooters, space shooters, ninja shooters, spy shooters, and, that's right, zombie shooters. This may not be that exciting for anyone who's grown up with this type of thing, but my family has always been frugal out of necessity, and I'd never even owned a TV. I indulged in these games like a fat kid indulges in sugar-glazed carbs, and to be honest, I got really good, unless Carmelle played me (she hoarded the good weapons and always kicked my ass, but I mean, I let her. Partially.).

Even though the apartment is kind of obnoxiously small sometimes (Carmelle used to joke how her dorm room was bigger, and I didn't want to start anything by reminding her the only reason she had such a big dorm was because her roommate was bulimic and had to go back to rehab midway through the semester), we could sit for hours and play these games in these expansive terrains and forget all about how cramped up we were, and how long it'd been since we'd last seen each other naked.

All of this to say, I am an excellent shot.

So when Renni Ramirez and I are seconds away from becoming the main course for an extended family of very hungry zombies popping out of the parking lot like the asphalt is spawning them, I let myself panic for a fraction of a second, and then I suck it up and take action.

I let Renni pull me along as I lift up my injured leg, wincing at the stab of fresh pain, and hop along, trying to wedge my fingers under the heel of my Skecher.

"What are you doing?" Renni sounds annoyed.

"Keep moving," I say, a little more frantically than I'd intended.

The moaning becomes like a roar the closer the zombies get. They must be strategizing instinctively or telepathically or something because they've got us surrounded in a quickly tightening circle. The nearest one is about eight yards ahead and to the left of us. Of course, I could be wrong about this; I haven't checked behind us yet.

"Almost there," Renni assures me, gripping my waist like a vise as she pull-pushes me along.

I nod but it just looks like a consequence of all the hopping. Finally, I dig my fingers around the heel of the shoe between my socked foot and the tennis shoe fabric and pull my swelling foot free. When the cold air hits my foot it's the best feeling I've had all day, a born-again feeling, a hot bath after a crappy day feeling. But I can't relish in it for too long. I scan the parking lot for the most expensive looking car. There, three parking lanes over near the return cart corral: a silver Beemer. I sure hope I am right about this; between the two of us, I only have three more chances, three more shoes.

Like I said, I don't have to worry about my aim.

Adjusting for my inability to put weight on my now shoeless right leg, and the velocity of my hop-hobble, I pull back my right shoulder, kiss the cloudless sky for luck, squint into my last hope, and chuck the Skecher as hard as I can at the Beemer. It connects with the windshield, the impact drowned by the zombie moans, and bounces onto the minivan parked next to it. And my luck is even better than I'd thought: both the Beemer and the minivan have car alarms, and both blare out into the day now.

Alarmed and intrigued by this new set of boisterous blinks, beeps, and blarts, the zombies pause in their travels and, one by one, begin to peel off their original trajectories and scrape-crawl-limp-shuffle away to investigate this new development.

Renni shakes her head, and I can't tell if she's smiling or grimacing.

Our path clear, we're at her parking space in about ten seconds. She leans me up against her pale green hybrid and plunges a hand into a pocket of her camo pants.

"This a rental?" I inquire of the Hybrid.

She sneers at the car and blows air out through her lips, like *ppbbbblltt*, which makes me laugh. "Not mine. That's mine."

She points to the space she's standing in: a motorcycle. I'm no expert on models or makes, but it looks like a Harley Davidson to me.

"Is it a rental?" I ask, joking.

Renni swings her leg over the bike like a pro and leans back to open one of the saddle bags. She pulls out a solid black helmet. "Come here. I only got one."

There's not a lot of space on the back seat of the bike, barely a seat really, so I have to sit pretty close to her, my pelvis pretty much wedged into the small of her back. She bonks the helmet over my head and the world is muted by the insulation. Her scent engulfs me, I almost swoon. She ate chicken salad for breakfast. Somehow, the sunglasses she'd clipped to the bust line of her dress before this all began have survived; I watch her through the lightly fogged plastic of the helmet's visor as she puts on the shades, gives me one more look and quirk of a smile, then turns back and kicks on the motor.

She doesn't have to tell me to hold on tight. I might be kind of a dummy, but I'm also an opportunist. My arms are snug around her waist before we're barely doing twelve miles per hour to clear the parking lot.

Zombies *whoosh* by on all sides of us; some reaching out to us, others still fooled by my ruse, fruitlessly banging away on the windows of the Beemer and minivan. I can't count them all. As we zoom by other closed-up shops along the strip, I strain to see in their windows to find survivors, but my eyesight's not functioning too well behind this visor. It could use a good washing.

The lights are out at the four-way stop leading to the freeway on ramp, and there are other cars around, obediently waiting their turn to pass through. Oblivious to the massacre playing out only a block down the road. I hope no one is thinking of going shopping today.

We speed up the on ramp. The rushing wind is cold against my exposed skin, but it feels good along my injured leg, which has heated up by the minute. I think of infection, and then I think of Infection. If those things are zombies, and if any zombie lore can be said to be consistent, it is always that once bitten, you become one. Undead. Living dead. Zombie. Me.

The more I try to convince myself that isn't going to be happening—none of this is happening; it's a dream, just like Cherry said—the more solid Renni Ramirez's back feels against my chest, the harder I hold her. This is real. Somehow, this is real.

I have to tell Carmelle.

My cell phone is still in my pocket. A blue hospital sign careens by on the side of the road, and seconds later we are slowing down to take the off ramp. Once we get to the hospital, have a chance to clean up and get some antibiotics, send someone out for Cherry and Brad and to put down those poor bastard zombies, I will find a quiet corner of a room somewhere and call Carmelle. I wonder if she experienced her own attack, or if she's just calmly going about her business, shelving dildos and alphabetizing hardcore DVDs, like normal.

The freeway exits onto a commercial road that rolls us by three used-car dealerships, two gas stations, four Taco Bells (what is the deal with that?), and a lone bait n' tackle shop (the nearest lake is fifteen miles southwest of here, technically in Indiana). I try to make out the activity on the street or in the parking lots of these places, to see if anyone is fleeing for their lives or hobbling in search of brains, but all seems normal, even calm. We turn right, then take a slight left, and we're here, the large brown four-story building of Saint Mercy hospital. I was actually born here twenty-two years ago, but then it was called Francis Bacon Care Center, so I'm not sure if it counts as the same place anymore.

There's the normal amount of hurried activity around the entrance to the emergency room. Renni Ramirez pulls right up to the double doors, parking her hog on the sidewalk and killing the engine. I pull off the helmet, sad to let her scent go, but grateful to be able to hear fully again. An ambulance pulls up pretty close behind us, and the two attendants open the back door and usher out an older gentleman with an oxygen mask glued to his face. They walk him into the building and glare at us as a nurse comes out the doors, headed for us.

"Excuse me, you can't park here," she says. She waves agitated hands at us and frowns.

"It's an emergency," Renni calmly explains. "My friend's injured."

She takes off her sunglasses and wipes a hand through her wind-tousled hair. The messier it is somehow the sexier it is. I have to force myself to stop looking at her.

The nurse gasps at the sight of Renni's broken nose, and then blinks a few extra times as she realizes who the nose belongs to. "You're both hurt," she tells us, like it's news to us.

"Seems like," Renni says, swinging a leg over the bike and helping me off.

"Okay, well, I'll get a wheelchair for the girl," the nurse offers. "You just pull that thing over here, away from the entrance." She points to a spot near the bicycle racks and heads back inside.

Renni stands me up. "You good?"

I give her the okay sign with my fingers, and close my eyes to keep from getting dizzy. But of course this doesn't help, it only makes me forget I'm standing and causes some troublesome rumblings in my stomach, so I have to open them again. The nurse wheels out a chair for me and eases me into it. Renni comes back over and surveys the parking lot.

"Pretty average day here?" she asks the nurse.

"Oh, no day at the emergency room is average," she says, but she's oddly cheery about it. "Just this morning we had a man come in with the strangest...predicament."

We talk as we walk (and I roll). I think the breath catches in both Renni and my throats when the nurse brings up this strange man, but she goes on. "He had this...well...he'd inserted an object into someplace...into an Exit Only, let's say."

"But he was alive?" I want to make sure.

The nurse laughs, a far more jovial sound than her stern face would make her seem capable of delivering. "He's fine, a little embarrassed, but the doctor was able to retrieve the item."

"What was it?" Renni wants to know. I look at her like, *really?* She shrugs and gives my shoulder a little punch.

"A little plastic toy car." The nurse shakes her head. "It was his son's. We went ahead and let him think we believed his story of having slipped stepping out of the shower and falling on it. He'll be back next week with a similar 'accident,' ten to one."

We reach the nurse's station at the head of the emergency room waiting area. There actually aren't too many people waiting around: a forty-ish mother with her two young boys sitting under the television in the corner, flipping through magazines; a be-flannelled mid-thirties lumberjack type holding an oil-stained rag over his hand in one of the center seats; and a sixty-some-odd-year-old couple holding hands in the seats nearest the entrance doors.

An identical nurse behind the station hands Renni a clipboard and a pen. The other nurse lets go of my wheelchair and says, "You'll have to fill out those forms. It's procedure."

"It's the emergency room." Renni enunciates like she's speaking to a child with a head injury. "Some crazed junky bit a hole in her leg; it's actively inviting infection the longer you refuse to treat it. She needs to be tested for hepatitis, among other things. I'm sure you can get started on her while I take care of these formalities, hm?"

That's the most amount of words I've ever heard Renni Ramirez string together at one time, in real life or on screen. Her characters aren't exactly known for being verbose. And she's speechifying on behalf of me. I feel like a proud parent…but in a reverse-Oedipal way.

"Well, but," the nurse behind the counter starts, "Is she covered under your insurance?"

Renni plunges a hand into the side pocket of her camo pants and pulls out her wallet. She takes out her insurance card and hands it over. "Yeah, she's my cousin."

"I thought she was your friend?" The other nurse says.

"We get along," Renni says.

"This insurance company only gives coverage to immediate family," the counter nurse says.

"Yeah, she's my sister."

"But you just said…."

"Sometimes I don't like her too much so I pretend she's my cousin to piss her off."

"But...."

"Hey look, guys—I'm bleeding!"

While they were occupied in their verbal battle, I surreptitiously drove my fingers into my bandage until I almost blacked out from the pain and felt the bandage grow soggy with my blood. I am the queen of quick distractions. Also, I may need to throw up.

Finally recognizing the urgency of the situation, nurse number one takes the reins of my wheelchair and pushes me through some swinging doors into the halls of the emergency wing. Briefly, I regret not saying goodbye to Renni—or thank you, or please sign my breasts—because I have a feeling she won't be sticking around, with me or this crazy, zombie-infested town.

The nurse leads me to a single empty room, lays a paper gown out on the roll-away hospital bed and tells me to get changed. "I'll have a doctor in to examine you in just a minute," she says, turns on her heel military style, and she's gone.

Alone, the world becomes as quiet as it was inside Renni's motorcycle helmet. Slowly I climb out of the wheelchair and lie on top of the paper clothes on the thin, uncomfortable mattress of the bed. This is all the energy I can manage. I lie there on my stomach, fingers clenching, releasing, clenching the pillow that is just centimeters away from my head but I don't have the energy to slide it beneath me. I'm not Superman. Here without any distractions, in this swollen bubble of illusory safety and false normalcy, I can finally stop listening out for everyone and everything else and just listen to my body. Oh, joy.

My brain has been rightly ignoring the pain in my leg because it's like information overload; my nerves can only deliver so many messages at once. The whole thing feels like it's steeped in lava that is at once volcanically hot and iceberg cold. The icy hot stab of pain shoots all the way up from the bite and spider-webs out over my chest, along the back of my throat, and up into my brain, specifically right behind my eyes. The Advil I'd taken earlier soothed my fever some, but it's gonna take some extra-strength prescription shit to knock this bitch out. Speaking of knocking things out, I've noticed my eyelids have become increasingly heavy, and that even though the blackness of closing my eyes brings with it the intense urge to vomit, I keep closing them. Close, open, close, open. Like prolonged blinking.

Suddenly I cease to be aware of anything, not my body or the pain. I pass out.

While my body lies there doing its unconscious healing thing bodies are wont to do, these other things are happening:

...Renni Ramirez sits in the waiting room, ostensibly filling out insurance forms while chewing on the pen cap (later bid over by the nurses and orderlies, finally won by Thomas T. Thomas for $25 and two tickets to the monster truck rally on Thursday), trying to figure out which sounds better: "By the way, there's a horde of zombies causing some shit at the strip mall down yonder. Might want to check into that." Or: "A group of smelly men assaulted me in the strip mall down yonder, could you be a dear and go defend my honor? Bring some guns!"

...A group of three male doctors huddle behind the swinging doors to the back quarters of the emergency room, spying through the glass at the famous actress in the spotted blue sundress and navy camo pants, alternately convincing themselves it can't be her and upping each other's bribes for the chance to set her broken nose.

...Brad and Cherry hold each other in the manager's office of Ashbee's, telling themselves their closeness is born only out of their need for warmth, even though the zombie outbreak has had little to no effect on the quality of the air conditioning. He listens out for any strange sounds, prepared to start piling chairs in front of doors, because it's the only thing he can think of to do; she listens to her heart beating, and to his heart beating, and wonders why it has taken her so long to notice how ripped his pectoral muscles are beneath his unflattering Ashbee's vest.

...My brain regurgitates previously absorbed facts about zombies—namely, that if you are bitten by a zombie, you become a zombie—into a soup of my deepest seated anxieties—surrounding my body image, my lack of college education, how I killed my gerbil that one time because I left the cage open and it got out and I sat on it , and Carmelle—and feeds it back into my dreamscape, so that while my body repairs itself, I am treated to this fun adventure: I'm having sex with Carmelle, she's on top, straddling me with her fingers between my legs and my hands on her bouncing breasts, and

I'm moaning, but not in a sexy oh-yeah-baby-do-it-just-like-that way, and then I say out loud (or in my brain), "You look delicious. Let me taste you." And bouncing, straddling Carmelle laughs because she thinks I'm being sexy when really I am just hungry, because next thing either of us knows, I'm clinging to her left breast with my teeth and ripping out her nipple, tying my tongue around the nerve endings as if it were a maraschino cherry. She falls back, clutching her bleeding chest, saying over and over, "I knew it, I knew it." My gerbil runs across my bed and I step on it. The scene shifts and I'm dragging my rotting feet down the street, arms out in the horror movie classic zombie strut, and some hot punk girls across the street point at me and laugh. One of them says, "She's fat."

When I slog out of this fever dream, I lie perfectly still and keep my eyes closed, savoring the blackness, the solitude. Only vaguely do I hear the sound of people's voices, and only slowly do I recognize the voices are coming from a television or radio program. I can't make out exact words, but one program employs a laugh track (or a very lubricated live audience) before the channel changes. It occurs to me that someone must be in the room with me in order to change these channels, and that's when I have to start remembering where I am and why I'm here. I open my eyes.

It's a slightly different hospital room; this one has a window that looks out onto the parking lot. It's a single room with its own bathroom off to my right, and a small TV anchored to the wall in the corner. In front of which, Renni Ramirez stands, pointing a black remote at it like a magic wand, shaking it in agitation.

She's still here.

For a few minutes, I just watch her. I haven't moved at all yet, except to turn my head slightly, and she's so intent on flipping the channels of the television that she hasn't noticed I'm awake. She's pulled her hair back into a wavy ponytail tied up in a plain rubber band she probably got off one of the nurses; fine brown wisps tickle the sides of her face, her ears. With her hair up, the bulk of her neck is exposed, and I spend thirty-seven seconds studying the contours of this alone, how neatly it curves into her collarbone, how delicately it moves when she swallows. I admire the vibrancy of her tanned, brown skin—which, this close up, I can see has been slightly freckled by the sun in some places, like along her elbow—and how well it complements her sundress and camo pants. An odd combination that she works with enviable confidence. Somehow, her outfit has suffered not a drop of blood. And there, her sunglasses still dangle comfortably against the bust of the dress. A bandage is now taped across the bridge of her nose, and the blood has been cleaned away. It's calming, the surreal effect of her presence here in this hospital room in the middle of Nowhere, Ohio, but also panic-inducing; it proves that the laws of probability no longer apply: As long as Renni Ramirez can stand next to your bedside and watch forty seconds of a *M*A*S*H* rerun, the dead can walk the earth.

Finally, I make a little waking-up noise—yawning wetly, fidgeting under the thin hospital blanket, crinkling the stupid paper gown someone has changed me into. I blink my eyes as if I've just opened them, and Renni is standing right next to my bed. Before I can greet her, she sticks a hand through the metal safety rail and clasps my hand, gently.

"Devin," she says, and her voice cracks. Her eyes look watery, red lines of exhaustion or stress cloud the milky whites, stabbing the deep brown irises. She swallows hard, creases appear on her forehead like omens, and she tries again, "Devin, it's bad."

I think so many things all at once that I think nothing at all. The fear in my eyes must be well communicated because she tightens her grip on my hand and a single tear escapes her eye, lingers on her cheek for support.

"There was nothing they could do, Devin," she says. "Your leg... they...they had to amputate."

I bolt upright and lunge for my legs, kicking off the blanket, and grasp my knee about the same time Renni's evil cackle cannonballs out of her. My face flushes, starting at the neck and steaming to my ears, as I pat both my good legs, one bandaged professionally now, the other perfectly fine all along.

"Good one," I say dryly, the words scratching my throat.

Renni pushes away from my bedside, still laughing, and wipes away the tear. "I had to do it, man."

There's a peach-colored pitcher and two Styrofoam cups on the bedside table near my IV. She pours water from the pitcher into one of the cups and hands it to me. "Thanks," I say, drinking.

"They don't just hire me for my stereotype," she says, and turns back around to try the television again.

"What are you doing?"

"Trying to get a local news station," she says, jamming buttons with her thumb.

"Try four."

She clicks over to the channel but it's nothing but the last vestiges of Sunday morning cartoons clinging to their final moments of air-time.

"This town does have one news van, right?" She leaves the channel where it is and throws the remote on the chair against the window, defeated. "I mean, they'd be covering that shit in the strip if there was anything to cover, right?"

"You sound like you think we hallucinated all of it."

She wipes nonexistent sweat from her neck and looks over at some invisible spot on the wall, as if remembering. "No, man, it happened."

"Didn't you tell someone about it, or call the police?"

"Sort of," she says. She rolls her eyes at my look of concern. "Look, I'm not gonna tell people some zombies just ate a couple of guys, okay. I told them there was a riot and that's how we both got hurt. They sent a couple of cars."

My mind flashes on Biff, innocently wandering into his death moments after relieving himself, woefully unprepared for what awaited him. I think of Cherry insisting the cops aren't equipped to deal with the impossible, and of the hordes that almost got us as we limped our way out of the parking lot. And suddenly I'm crying.

Crying makes me feel like I'm six years old, and I want to be six years old so I can hide my face under the blanket and sleep away the pain, cartoon voices in the background lulling me into a false sense of security that only needs to last until my well runs dry. But I can't hide under the blanket. I'm an adult. A blubbering, weak, foolish, near-crippled adult, crying in front of Renni Fucking Ramirez.

As if things couldn't get any more surreal, she swoops away my water cup before I can humiliate myself further by spilling it all over myself, and touches my face to wipe the tears off my cheeks with her thumbs. She crouches down next to me to be eye level, and runs her fingers through the tangles in my hair.

"It's okay," is all she says, and it's all she needs to say. I try hard to pull myself together, for her. I sniff back mucus, blink back eye gunk, lick the salt off my lips. Renni's hands move from my face to hold my hand, for real this time.

"That guy was your friend, huh?" She asks.

I shake my head. Then I nod. "He was my boss."

"You called him a bear."

I smile a little, which turns into a small laugh. "He kind of was."

"Yeah," Renni says. "I could see that."

We sit there in silence for a minute, remembering Biff Tipping, the Bear.

After a time, I ask her, "How's your nose?"

She crinkles her nose in a *Bewitched* way, and looks at it cross-eyed. "I can't really feel it anymore." With her free hand, the one not holding onto me, heavy and reassuring, she takes an orange bottle of pills out of her pocket. "Endocet. Can't pony up for the real stuff in Buttfuck, Ohio, I guess."

I smile at the wink in her voice, and tap my IV. "Must be pumping something pretty good into me. I can barely feel my leg anymore."

Unfortunately, I ruin the relative lightness of our moment by calling attention to my possible Infection. Honestly I've been trying not to think about it, but it's all I think about. And now that I've had that damn dream, all I think about is the leg, my poor underfoot gerbil, and those girls calling me fat (Who calls a zombie fat? Honestly!). There's an awkward moment where we both try not to look at my leg, and end up meeting each other's eyes, which is somehow even more awkward.

Luckily, Renni is adept at conversation starters. "I'm double jointed. Want to see?"

She shows me how she can pop her elbow out the wrong way, which enables her to twist her arm around at an ungodly angle. She can pop some bone in her wrist out too, to shift it while she spins her arm almost full circle on the hospital mattress. "Put your fingers there," she instructs, and I touch the bone as she twists her hand around. I can feel it pop, and then the sinews of tendons pushing it around. Her skin is hot, or my skin is, and I have to break contact before I start blushing again.

"That's just for you," she says, crossing her arms over the safety rail, no longer holding my hand, but it's okay. "No blogging."

"What makes you think I even have a blog?"

"Everyone has a blog," she says offhandedly.

"Well, no offense or anything, but I'll probably write about getting bit by a zombie before I mention your name." Dammit, Devin, back to the conversation-killer leg.

"All right, you need to take the zombie quiz," Renni says.

I just kind of look at her like she's lost it.

"First question: are you hungry?"

"What?" She raises her eyebrows at me. "I guess I could eat."

"Second question: are you hungry for brains?"

"I...don't think so." My mouth is kind of salivating, but it's more for the taste of cheese than anything else right now.

"Third question: Are you hungry for human flesh?"

"No," I say.

"Final test." She picks up my arm by the wrist and touches two fingers to the pulsing vein. "Oh look you're alive. Not a zombie." She drops my wrist back onto the bed dramatically. "Good enough for you?"

I just start laughing, I can't help it. We laugh together for a minute, and then I say, stupidly, "I'm glad you're here."

Her laugh kind of morphs into a snort and she looks down at her arms, once again crossed over the bedrail, and doesn't say anything.

In an effort to make things even more awkward, I continue to say more stupid things. "Why are you here, anyway? In Ohio?"

She snort-laughs again, and wipes at some phantom stray hairs on her forehead. "I was riding with someone. Supposed to do the coast-to-coast thing. He bailed in Virginia. I kept riding."

"At the store, you said you were waiting for someone."

"Yeah," she says, starting to trail off. "Think I waited long enough."

"Then why stay?"

She looks at me then, in a way that makes me want to avert my eyes; I have to pinch my thigh under the blanket to stay focused. Her mouth kind of crooks into a half-smile, her eyes narrow invitingly, she licks her lips and says, "Do you want me to go?"

You know, zombies didn't start out as the brain-eating cannibals we all know and love (in movies, anyway). They didn't even use to be free agents. They were like slaves of the mystic world, summoned by a witch or whatever the male version of witch is and given instructions on who to maim or kill or frighten into an early grave. According to some fanzine I read in high school, George Romero changed all that with his zombies in the now classic *Night of the Living Dead* movie. His zombies rose up from the grave of their own mysterious volition, and they were spurred on not by evil conjurors but by a deep, unending need to *feed*. I'm not sure when the once-bitten lore became a zombie standard (following down the well-trodden path of vampires and werewolves), if it was Romero too, or something older. I don't even know for sure if the dude who bit me today was a zombie or just some skeezed-out old homeless guy gone psychotic due to lack of meds (but how to explain the small horde waiting for us in the parking lot?), but I am sure that he did bite me. Hard and hungry enough to tear out a mouth-sized chunk of flesh. And if he was a zombie, soon I will be too. So, there's no real reason to lie to Renni Ramirez now, right?

"No," I tell her, bravely maintaining eye contact. "I'd prefer it if you stayed."

Another reason I know this is not a movie, or a dream, or a hallucination: no one comes into the room to interrupt our moment at just the right time. Seriously, a nurse should have walked in by now, somebody, so we can both relax here. But no, we have to sit here with our words hovering between us (mostly my words, all stupid and formal—"I'd prefer it if you stayed"—Jesus Christ), both of us too stubborn to break eye contact or the silence, just kind of looking at each other, trying to decide how much of this is real, and how much we're making up as we go.

Finally, Renni breaks the spell by gracefully punching me in the knee. "Hey, you should call those coworkers of yours. See if they made it out okay."

"Oh, yeah," I say, feeling slightly ashamed that I hadn't thought to do that immediately. I pat down my paper hospital gown until it dawns on me that I'm wearing a paper hospital gown. "They took my clothes."

Renni rolls her eyes and pushes away from the bed. My clothes are folded in a neat pile on top of the chair by the window. Renni ruffles through the khaki pockets and lobs the phone onto my lap.

Cherry answers on the first ring. "Devin! You're alive!"

"You too," I say, less excitedly not because I'm not happy to hear her voice, but because it's just not my personality to let that kind of thing show.

"Oh my God, would you slow down? Drive like a sighted person, please!"

"Who are you talking to?" I ask. Renni is only half-listening to my side of the conversation, having picked up the remote and resumed her trolling of the television for breaking news.

"Bradley. He's driving like a maniac."

"So you guys made it out of Ashbee's?" I am the queen of stupid questions. Bow down, peons, bow down.

"Yeah, as soon as the sirens blew down the street, all the dead heads went nuts. They—"

"'Dead heads' sounds like you're talking about Grateful Dead fans."

"—What?"

"Just say zombies."

"Whatever." Cherry may not have appreciated my insight, but it got a cute little huff out of Renni. "All these police cars showed up, fire trucks, ambulances—I'm telling her, Brad, just drive!—all these cars with loud-ass sirens. They just drew the dea-zombies, drew the zombies like flies to sugar. We didn't stick around to see what happened next. We booked it out the loading dock and jumped into Brad's car and we were gone. Devin—you should call Carmelle."

My heart—at least Renni was right, I *am* still alive—double-times its beats. "Why?"

"We cut down Main Street—Brad's taking me to his uncle's place in Indiana, to get out of town until we know what's up, you know?— Anyway, we turned down Main Street, and, Devin, oh man—"

"Christ, Cherry, just fucking tell me." But I'm already kicking at the safety rail, trying to get up. My IV catches and I rip it out of the back of my hand. Kind of hasty; it hurts like a motherfucker.

From Cherry's end of the phone I hear Brad's hurried expletives. Cherry screams at him, "Shut up! I'm telling her! Okay, Devin, listen, I'm not saying it means anything—"

"Cherry!"

"There was a mob of them outside of the Onion. Zombies. It was like a crowd...uh...I couldn't see much, we were driving fast but, I couldn't see inside or anything, but...it looked like they were trying to get in. Devin—"

"Thanks, Cherry," I say, rushed. "I'm glad you're all right."

I hang up and finally untangle myself from the bed. The back of my hand is bruising quickly and dripping blood, but I ignore it. I ignore, too, Renni's look of concern and mild irritation, and the fact that my paper hospital gown has no back and I am wearing my pink cotton laundry day underwear that Renni can plainly see as I move around her to retrieve my clothes from the chair.

Behind me, she whistles like the clichéd construction worker. "Fancy."

"Shut up," I hiss and tug on my khakis. I'm trying to dial while I slip my shirt over the paper dress, but it's not working too well.

"Here," Renni steps forward to help me. "You're spazzing out. God, those clothes are ruined." They are covered in various stages of drying blood. "Take those off."

Renni Ramirez just told me to take off my pants. Now she is pulling her sundress over her head. I drop my phone.

Under her sundress, Renni wears—what else?—a white tank top with spaghetti straps, which I had earlier taken to be her bra straps. She must be wearing some kind of strapless bra or had some lift-and-stay surgery at some point because I can't say as I can make out any bra in the traditional sense. I can't look for too long, though, because she's holding the dress out to me.

"Put this on," she says. Then, with a smirk, "You dropped your phone."

I take the dress from her. "Turn around."

She arches an eyebrow at me, and I shoo her away with my back-hand. She shakes her head and smiles, and she turns around.

Quickly, I shed the scratchy paper gown and slip Renni's dress over my head and shoulders. She is taller than me, which is the only way to explain how her dress can fit so well around my decidedly more pear shaped body. I take a moment to smooth out the wrinkles, and breathe in her particular smell, tinged with a spot of cinnamon now, which I guess must be the work of her deodorant. The dress on, I scramble around on the floor for a minute and find my phone under the chair.

Renni says, "Can I turn back around now, princess?"

A little shiver passes through me that I attribute to some invisible draft. "Sure," I say, and find Carmelle's number in my contacts list.

"Looks good on you," Renni says, but I can't tell if she's joking.

Carmelle has her ring tone set up to play obnoxious trance-dance music into my ear in intermittent bursts. It plays the same two-point-five seconds of song on a loop about seven times before her voice-mail clicks on. "Fuck," I say before the beep comes, and flip the phone shut.

"What's up?" I forgot Renni has no idea what's going on.

"My girlfriend. Cherry said she drove past where she works and it's surrounded by zom…by rioters. She's not picking up her phone. Fuck." As I speak I'm frantically scanning the floor for my shoes, but they seem to be missing.

"Okay, call the store," Renni says.

I look at her. "You're a genius." I find the store's number and dial, but that phone just rings and rings and rings. "Goddammit." Whenever I swear this often, you know it must be bad.

"I can see your panty line," Renni says.

"What?" I look down at myself.

"Right there," Renni points to my butt. I crane my neck around to see. "Right here," Renni says, and pinches the line of fabric with her fingers and snaps it back against my skin.

Despite myself, I laugh like a giddy school girl, and play into it. "Stop! I can't see it."

"I can clearly see it," she says, and goes to snap it again. I bat her hand away and giggle some more, and then I drop my phone again. "Clumsy," Renni admonishes, and bends to pick it up. Our game has gotten the better of me and I do the dumbest thing I could possibly do in this situation: I spank Renni Ramirez's ass.

And *that's* when the nurse comes in.

"Oh, you're up!" the nurse chirps. She's wearing powder-blue scrubs and scuffing along in white paper shoes. She carries a purple clipboard on which I assume my medical information is clipped, and she marks something off with a red pen, then dips the pen beneath her wavy blond hair at the side of her face and it disappears behind her ear. Her big blue eyes shine only marginally brighter than her large white teeth. "How are you all feeling?"

Renni has bolted back up and, out of the corner of my eye, I see her drop my phone into the thigh pocket of her camo pants. To the nurse I say, "Fine."

"Wonderful! Oh no...." The nurse has seen that I've torn my IV out of my skin. "What happened here?"

I slap my left hand over the tiny hole in my right hand, which has already begun to scab over. "I didn't really need it anymore. I feel much better. I think I'm ready to go home."

The nurse, well-seasoned as she must be to all manner of please-let-me-go-home pleas, frowns and cocks her head at me like a curious puppy, as she deftly circles the bed, picks the remote up from the bedside table, and clicks off the buzzing television.

"Now let me just take a quick look at you, dear," she says, her use of the term "dear" grating on me because we are probably the same age, or close enough. "Then I'll tell the doctor you're feeling up to leaving, and we'll get you processed out. How would that be? Hm?"

Before I have a chance to respond dramatically, Renni swoops in with a distraction. "Did the police make it out to the site of the riot okay?"

The nurse looks at her, blinks a couple times to make sure she's awake, then proceeds professionally. "Oh that's right," she says, consulting the chart on her purple clipboard. "You all are the ones involved in the riot earlier today, aren't you. Well, don't you fret. We just received a call from a couple of our ambulance drivers and they are on their way here with a handful of injured, but other than that, activity at the strip mall seems to have trickled off by the time they got there."

Something catches in my chest. The same something that catches in Renni's as her voice struggles to move past it. "Injured?"

The nurse waves off her concern and plucks the pen back out from behind her ear. "You don't need to worry about that now. Now, come on, little missy." She pats the hospital bed. "Up you go. Let's have a look at you."

Just then, as if on cue, sirens rise like smoke in the distance. Renni and I both turn and move closer to the window, practically pressing our noses to the glass, our collective breath steaming up the pane. We don't see anything for several seconds as the siren's wail grows louder, but then there it is: the first ambulance, followed by a second, coming down the emergency ramp to the drop-off point in front of the entrance, which we have a clear shot of, only a few yards from us outside. Everything appears normal, except they're going too fast; both vehicles take the curve leading to the drop-off too fast, the first spins out, and the second barrels into it. From behind us, the nurse, hearing the crash, gasps, and steps up behind us, putting one hand on my back, and the other no doubt on Renni's back. *How brazen of her,* I think, and then I remember my own transgression just minutes before.

Outside, the ambulances have both stopped, perpendicular to each other, the side of one caved in, the front of the other letting off steam from its bashed-in engine. The drivers of both vehicles kick open their doors and jump out, running away from the scene, toward the hospital entrance. They meet a group of hospital workers—other EMTs, orderlies, nurses, drawn by the commotion—and pause only long enough to gesticulate wildly and scream, and then continue running by.

"What is going on?" the nurse breathes behind us.

Renni's arms shoot out and she manhandles the window open, ducks her head under it and shouts at the personnel, "Hey! Get away from the ambulance! Hey! Don't open those doors!"

But either they can't hear her over the still-screaming sirens, or they ignore her. Either way, they open the doors. And the zombies are on them like flies on sugar, to borrow a phrase. We watch for only a moment as the first orderly is topped by a young woman in church clothes—drab brown skirt to her ankles, plain yellow blouse spotted with blood, open and flapping in the wind, hair pulled back to reveal the ashen and leathery pull of her facial skin that I've come to recognize as the calling card of the dead, or undead, as the case may be. She tucks her knees into the orderly's armpits and rips into his skull with her incisors. Before anyone knows what's happening, another man leaps from the ambulance and brings down a nurse. At the second ambulance, an old man and a young boy fight over the dripping arm of a freshly amputated EMT woman.

The nurse behind us lets out a shriek more piercing than the wailing sirens, drops her clipboard, and flees the room. Half a second later, some alarm rips through the walls of the hospital, and we can hear distorted voices and hurried footsteps in the hall.

"You want to get to Carmelle, right?" Renni asks me, bringing me back to our current reality.

"Yeah, I have to," I say, believing it.

"Then we're going out the window," she says, and pops a leg effortlessly over the sill.

"Wait," I grab her shoulder—brazenly—and pull her back in. "It's insane out there. You can't go out there."

"My bike is right there." She points past the chaos and I see it, leaning on its kickstand near a bush by the entrance doors. "We can make it."

"As long as we're quiet," I echo her earlier warning to me.

She nods and smiles. "As long as it's worth it."

I don't answer her, but I push her through the window. I take three deep breaths, push out all questions of how crazy I am from my brain, and climb out behind her.

The zombies here in the hospital parking lot are simple enough to evade; they have their mouths full, after all. It's the horde outside The Sweet Onion that make my metaphorical balls shrivel up to dried prunes and escape back into my abdomen, from which they never descended because they're metaphorical.

Chapter 4

A Bird in the Hand Is Worth Two If You're Dead

As we head down Main Street, it is clear that something bad has happened. Like birds taking flight from trees during an antelope stampede, human people have spontaneously fled their morning routines or obligations, leaving behind their debris: coffee cups and half-eaten crullers at the outdoor cafés, dog-eared books strewn across the threshold of Mick's Used Books, renegade oranges rolling out of dropped shopping bags in the parking lot of Whole Foods. Cars have piled up in both lanes, causing blockages that Renni deftly snakes around by angling her bike onto the sidewalk. Doors to shops have carelessly been left open, strollers abandoned, and in two tragic instances, tiny yapping dogs left tied to fire hydrants. We start to hear the cause of this desertion before we see it: the underwater swell of the choking rattle, then the steady rise of the deep, monotone moan.

Renni pulls up behind a ditched Tacoma and cuts the bike's engine. Without the hog's loud roar, the horde's collective moan grows, even though they are still three blocks up. I see them surrounding the store at the corner of Main and Lemon Tree: twenty or thirty of them, pressed together like pigs in a slaughterhouse, flesh slapping, jaws dripping, hands clawing, mouths moaning. Fucking zombies.

Above their heads hangs the hand-painted wooden sign for The Sweet Onion: a white chalk drawing of an onion that used to just be a plain old onion when this was a mom-and-pop grocery store, but now has a face—one arched cartoon brow, one suggestively winking eye, a touch of red to mark two innocently bashful cheeks. The owners of the now porn shop—excuse me, adult store—decided to keep the name and original sign, with those slight alterations to the onion, and this: a slogan painted in sweeping calligraphy that reads, "Layers of Fun!"

Renni looks at me over her shoulder. "What do you want to do?"

"Go in," I say. Carmelle is trapped inside that store, and maybe if it were still a grocery store I wouldn't have to worry too much about her—what better place to hole up during a zombie attack, right? Except maybe a hospital (well, not the one we just came from)—but racks of hentai DVDs and variously flavored lube aren't going to sustain her for long. Besides that, there's a huge blacked-out window in the front wall of the store that won't stand up to those undead fists pounding on it all day.

"All right, Rambo," Renni says, "You want to charge in, bare fists flying? Be my guest."

Stupidly, I look at my hands, clench my fists a few times, then drop them at my sides. "You're right, we need a distraction."

She shakes her head, all-knowing. "Not gonna be enough this time. Too many of them. And whatever's in there, they want it bad. Listen."

I listen. She's right. Aside from their own slobbering moans, there's a plethora of natural and man-made alarms sounding off all over these blocks: dogs barking, televisions left on in storefront windows, car engines running, a few car alarms going off. This group of zombies is a hell of a lot more focused than the last group we faced (well, evaded).

"Okay," I nod, thinking. "Okay, then…."

"Weapons," Renni says. "We need lots and lots of weapons. Guns, preferably."

"I don't have a gun," I say, like she's nuts.

She takes her sunglasses off specifically to roll her eyes at me. "Are you kidding me? I've seen at least twelve pick-ups sporting truck nuts in just these last few blocks alone. Look, look right there." She points to the tailgate of the Tacoma in front of us. Sure enough, hanging from the back bumper like an afterthought, a bright blue plastic scrotum. "The ratio of truck nuts to guns and ammo stores in a town this small has got to be at least six to one."

Her logic is sound. "There is one over on Geary Street. And if you open a savings account at Third National, they give you a free hunting rifle."

She laughs at me and kickstarts the hog. "We'll try Geary first."

Geary is a few streets over, this block abandoned as well, though not quite as hurriedly. Quick Shot Guns & Ammo shares a rectangular parking lot with two other stores: a Check & Go, and Quick Shot Liquors. Some years ago there was talk of putting in a Quick Shot Mini Golf course across the street, but the town ultimately decided against adding to the confusion.

Lucky for us, whoever runs Quick Shot Guns also ran away when the zombies attacked. All we need to get in is the brick Renni has somehow managed to find and is now lobbing at the front window. As it shatters, an alarm goes off, and I scream, "Are you crazy?"

"Not a bad thing if the cops show up, is it?" Renni shrugs, kicks away some excess glass with her combat boot, and steps over the sill and into the store.

I have to get used to the new rules of this sudden reality. Alarms are okay as long as no zombies are around, or if you're trying to distract zombies. Breaking and entering is okay as long as it is in service to taking down zombies. Killing is okay as long as the people are already dead. Check, check, and oh God I think I'm gonna puke.

A wave of nausea slams into me as I gingerly climb over the sill, avoiding the broken glass shards. Once on the floor I have to kneel down to fight back the urge to vomit, but I pretend to be inspecting the hand guns in the window display. I can hear Renni in the store behind me, picking up guns and clicking their chambers open, then opening drawers behind the counter, rummaging for bullets.

When she comes back over to me, I stand up. She hands me a twelve-gauge pump action shotgun. "You okay?"

"Sure," I burp, and wipe my mouth. Renni looks at me dubiously, but I take the shotgun.

"Ever shoot before?" She asks.

I open the extended magazine and load up six shells from the box Renni holds out to me, slap the mag back in place and load a round into the chamber. "Buck hunting trips every other summer since I was ten."

"Must have a pretty cool dad," she says.

I grab the box of ammunition from her. "My mom took me."

We load up, filling a backpack with extra rounds and packing two handguns apiece, one .22 rifle with a sight for Renni, and my trusty rosewood shotgun. In addition, Renni insists we carry mêlée weapons: for her, two butterfly knives, a hatchet she shoves through her belt loop, and a break-glass-only-in-emergencies axe, for which she fashions a sort of sling from her belt and straps it to her back; for me, an eight-inch hunting knife safely secured in a leather sheath tied around my waist with light nylon rope, two pair of brass knuckles—wear one now, save one for later—and police-issue baton secured to my back with the same rope.

I feel encumbered, but I also feel empowered. Then I think about all the carnage we're about to expose ourselves to—we're about to cause—and how all the zombies we're about to bash in—if they really are zombies—were all once people.

"What happened, do you think?" I ask Renni as we're loading up her bike's saddle bags with extra guns and ammo.

"With what?"

I gesture to the world with my eyes. "With them. The zombies."

Renni looks around at nothing in particular, then back at me. "What always happens: someone got stupid, or bored, or creative. Voilà."

"You think someone *made* the zombies?"

"I don't know. Let's hear your explanation."

I look around at the same nothing as Renni, and come back with just as much of an idea. "I don't have one."

"Great." Renni drops her leg over the bike. "Try Carmelle one more time."

I dial her cell and then the store. Nothing.

Renni tosses me her bike helmet. "Saddle up, partner."

It takes a minute to get back to The Sweet Onion on the corner of

Main Street and Lemon Tree Lane. While Renni drives us there I think of exactly several things, plus one:

1. In the hours (two or three at the most, though I haven't consulted a timepiece lately) since meeting Renni Ramirez I have stopped referring to her by her full name—Renni Ramirez—in my head. It feels strange that her name should feel so familiar to me now, but then again, I do have her blood under the skin of my knuckles. Everything's relative.

2. Stranger still, I haven't referred to Renni Ramirez out loud to her face as anything—not Renni, or even "Hey You." I haven't had cause to scream it in alarm or fear either, so I'll count this one as a plus.

3. If Brad and Cherry hook up as a result of all of this, I will shit a brick. But they'll probably pull a *Speed* and decide relationships based on intense situations (or sex) never last, and everything will be ruined by the sequel (which will bomb).

4. I really want some chocolate-covered bacon, which makes me think I must be about to start my period.

5. How shitty would it be to die while on your period? Although I think everyone shits themselves at the moment of total body shutdown, but even so. Unseemly.

6. What if Renni and I end up kissing?

7. I met Carmelle long before she started working at The Sweet Onion, even before I knew she was a stripper, at a frat party off campus. She was outside by the pool, dancing despite the music from inside having mostly faded out here. Her hair was loose and streaming around her shoulders, which were bare in her black spaghetti-strap dress. She held her shoes in one hand and her red plastic beer cup in the other. She was maybe a little drunk, as was I, which was the only reason I approached her. "Want to swim?" I asked. There were a few couples in the pool, doing the opposite of swimming—by which I mean they were having sex, or something close to it; and one guy off in the far corner, peeing like a cherubic fountain.

"Do you have a car?" she asked me.

I drove her home and she was silent most of the way, but it wasn't far and I didn't mind listening to her breathing. I stopped outside her dorm building, tires crunching over glass from the street lamp someone had previously vandalized. This wasn't my car; I had borrowed it from my friend Darryl who was out of town for the weekend as payment for feeding his mom's thirteen cats—all Siamese, nearly identical but she could tell them apart—so I was a little bit worried that Carmelle would puke in it.

I leaned over to undo her seatbelt and she leaned her nose into my hair and I heard her smell me. Then she grabbed my left wrist. "What's that?"

She'd noticed my tattoo. "It's an emotional beet." It was a little cartoon beet, more like a red turnip, pounding its head with Mickey Mouse gloved hands, and crying overly large cartoon tears, surrounded by motion lines to indicate its shaking.

"A what?"

"I took this creative writing class last semester and some guy used the term 'emotional beat,' B-E-A-T, and I thought of this."

"What's an emotional B-E-A-T?"

I shrugged. "Something the class thought all my stories lacked."

"Jesus Christ," she said, and I thought she'd go then, just pop open the door and roll right out, but instead she grabbed my head with her clammy hands. "Come here."

I thought it was a one-night stand, but she answered her phone when I called the next day and we went out for coffee.

8. Renni hasn't noticed my tattoo, or if she has, she hasn't mentioned it. There has been a lot of blood flying around and dead people walking the streets to distract from it though.

Speaking of blood, we are back at our spot behind the Tacoma. Once again, Renni cuts the engine, then hops off. She takes a second to adjust the weapons on her person, check the sight of her rifle, and clip her sunglasses to the bust of her tank top (which reveals more cleavage than the dress had—or does on me). The sound of the zombies' incessant moaning is almost white noise, and now there's a smell, like wet cement and festering dog poop. I dismount the bike.

"Here's the plan," Renni says, pointing the barrel of her rifle at the building directly across from The Sweet Onion. "Those look like apartments above that deli. I'm going to break in and cover you from there. Don't go in until I've cleared a path. Got it?"

"Renni," I say out loud, testing the taste of it on my tongue, memorizing the vibrations it makes against my throat as my larynx pushes out the air.

She looks at me, expectant. I realize more must be said than just her name. But my brain can't settle on any one thing, the nausea returns in the center of me, my leg begins to heat up (or I begin to notice the heat that's always been there), and my sphincter closes up tight, so that the only thing that comes out next is a softly blurted, "Ramirez," trailing enough on the final syllable to sound prophetic.

Renni does all of this in the same second, like some sexy gorgeous flirtation gymnast: she curls her lip into her signature smirk, rests the butt of her rifle on her jutting hip, pulls the rubber band out that holds her hair together, shakes out the voluminous honey-brown waves, and says, "No formalities now, sugar tits. We've already been intimate." And just to emphasize the memory, she slaps my thinly covered ass as she walks by me.

The heat has moved from my leg into my face. If I had no words before, I've certainly lost them indefinitely now. I follow a few paces behind Renni, trying not to look at her butt the whole way, trying, instead, to picture Carmelle's butt, which is slightly smaller and not as solid, but feels good between my teeth and tastes like the baby powder she always freshens up with before bed. Before she passed her silent embargo on sex, that smell would arouse the shit out of me, but now, when she's right there next to me reading or clipping her nails or popping her gum while she reads and clips her nails, doing anything but touching me, I just resent it.

We slink along the wall of the deli, keeping one eye on the zombie horde and one eye on the shadows. Nothing moves that isn't supposed to—well, except for all the dead people.

Even though our voices will most likely be drowned out by the zombie moans and car alarms and barking dogs and—is that a helicopter?—we still dare not speak this close to so many zombies. Renni points to herself, makes a little ascending walking motion with her fingers through the air, mimes popping off a few rounds, then points to me, and points to The Sweet Onion.

I shoot her a thumbs up. She disappears into the deli. I wait in its cold shadow, observing the slovenly attack across the street. There are three lines of zombies, one overlapping the other, the zombies in the third line attempting to climb the backs of the zombies in the second line, and so forth. Each one ignores all the others, as if only it existed, only it *can* exist—it, and its food trapped inside. These are decidedly less fresh than the ones we met in Ashbee's parking lot. I can tell this by the maggots flopping out of their ears, the spiders laying eggs in their hair, the flies forming a cloud around their heads, and by the pungent stink of poop. Judging from the majority of the attire donned by the predominantly male crowd—gray or brown suits that may have once been light blue or black, conservative low cut skirts and long-sleeved blouses—and the amount of dirt that crumbles down the mountain of their shaking bodies as they thump-thump-thump the shatter-proof glass, these zombies had once been people who died long enough ago to have been buried.

One of the zombies in the back row falls to his knees as his head explodes. His liquefying brain matter sprays a fellow zombie, who does not even turn around, and the one's skull ruptures and his knees give out. I can't even hear the report of the rifle until she's taken out six of them and their moaning has thinned. It's about that same time that some of them start to turn around, and notice me.

I have seven rounds in the shotgun and a nylon rope belt holding onto a couple mêlée weapons. If the zombies were attacking one by one, I might not be afraid to start firing, might be able to take down enough of them, with the help of Renni's sniper bullets, to make it safely to the door. But the zombies choose this moment to recognize each other and shift seamlessly into their mob mentality. More than twenty of them come at me at once, moving impossibly fast now that my scent is on their tongues (the ones that still have their tongues, at any rate).

I tuck the shotgun under my shoulder, two-fist it and squeeze. The shot blows apart the nearest zombie, whose squishy bits splatter in all directions, including onto me. Another shot takes out a woman whose family apparently had her buried in an American-flag-patterned jumpsuit. The third shot only clips the leg off one, who continues to pull itself along by his arms, and then I have to grip the still-hot barrel and swing the shotgun like a baseball bat at the nearest zombie jaw and make a mad dash for the door because there are too many of them too close now.

I scream as a callused, decayed hand clamps down on my arm and then falls away under the pressure of Renni's bullet. I run across the street, not looking behind me, faintly hearing the moaning, the rolling thunder report of the rifle, and the bottle-cap popping of hollow skulls exploding.

At the door, I tug and twist and push and pull at the handle, hoping the zombies couldn't get in because they'd forgotten how to use their thumbs, but no luck, the door is locked. Then there's pain in my left shoulder and I whip back and around but the damn thing is on there good, and more are coming. I slam back into the door, hard enough to knock the zombie's teeth loose, dislodging him from my body, and stomp on his head without looking. My foot lodges into his skull, but before I can process how gross this is, I have to turn back to the onslaught and fire three blind rounds to buy myself time. Clunkily, I shake the zombie slop off my bare foot, pretending the slimy, inky brain goop is just rain water. I turn to the door, release a wild animal-slash-Xena Warrior Princess battle yodel, level the shotgun at the glass, and fire.

Inside, I have to move fast, not only because I just blew a large human or zombie-sized hole in the only barrier keeping them out and any moment now they're gonna come scraping in after me, but also because my adrenaline rush is quickly losing out to my exhaustion and rapid blood loss.

I move through the debris of phallic sex toys and blow-up vaginas, to the opposite side of the store where the cash register is. Behind the counter is the door to the office and I slam into it, bad shoulder first, and nearly pass out. Everything gets kind of fuzzy at the edges, and I hear the deadbolt snap back and watch the doorknob turn.

"Fuck off, we're fucking closed," some naked chick yells into my face. Her eyes widen as she takes me in. I feel myself peeing and try to pretend it's just zombie brain goop. "Oh my God," she breathes.

Behind her, Carmelle, wrapped in a plastic Twister game mat where all the colored circles are shaped like dicks, slides into view.

When she sees me, the mat almost falls off her. She opens her mouth but doesn't say anything. I step back once, then my brain overheats, my vision goes wobbly, and I collapse.

Chapter 5

dead if you do, dead if you don't

THE THING ABOUT ALL THIS IS I SAW IT COMING. LONG before this, before I'm splayed out in a puddle of my own urine, the dangling breasts of my girlfriend's lover nipping against my nose as she catches my head before it can crack against the tiles (great reflexes, bet she's a gymnast in the sack) and flexes the muscles in her thighs to ease my dead weight onto the dirty floor (who has time to sweep up when there's fresh pussy to be eaten, am I right?). I saw it coming the first night she rolled away from me, and when I tried to spoon her, she mumbled something about cramps, and then the next night she didn't smell like baby powder, she smelled like honey almond perfume, the kind of scent you want to eat up quick, lick the last sugary dregs from the corners of your mouth and go back for seconds, thirds, a lifetime supply. And I got a reminder the other night when, with a sigh, she unzipped my pants and gave me a gift so obligatory after two months of nothing that I couldn't even get off. And now this naked chick, she smells like honeyed almonds; her breath smells like honeyed almonds, her hair, her fingers. And coconut. Where the hell's that coming from?

So if I knew it, if I saw it coming, why do I faint? Well, I knew it, but I forgot it, I let myself forget it. A rough patch, I thought, and maybe it is only me, it *is* only me, she'll come around, or I will, it will all work out. Then the zombies, then Renni Ramirez, then Biff. It could be the blood loss too. It could be the image of them, curled up warm and fucking under a novelty Twister game mat in here, while zombies maim and kill their friends and neighbors out there, until those zombies are magnetized to this pot, to The Sweet Onion, because they can sense the flesh inside, heated up and ready to serve.

Mostly, I'm gonna go with: it's the look on Carmelle's face. She looks hurt, like I slapped her with my presence, like I betrayed her by interrupting her affair. I'd be pissed if she looked annoyed, crushed if she looked happy (like, *finally, I can stop pretending*), and numb if she looked sorry. But she looks pained, physically pained, to have had me see her wrapped up in the scent of another woman.

And so I pee (my body just lets go), and so I faint (my mind just follows suit), and so I've got a pretty good vantage point when Renni Ramirez races into the store, and in a blur of misunderstanding, pistol whips the naked woman standing over me with the butt of her thirty-eight special.

"Mudderfudder," naked lady yelps as she falls back, holding her mouth. It reddens but doesn't bleed.

"Sorry," Renni says, sounding hard. "Thought you were a zombie."

Renni's heroic entrance didn't go as easy on her outfit as our previous evasion tactics had. Her white tank top is gray with various zombie matter, her navy camo pants spotted black with something that may have been blood or embalming fluid at one time. Her bare arms are streaked with scratches—that's right, don't your fingernails continue to grow after you die? Built-in mêlée weapons, sneaky zombie fucks—but I can't see any bites. I'm coming around from my haze, and the vertigo is wearing off.

"Get 'em all?" I ask her. She flicks her eyes to me briefly and nods quick, then returns her attention, her stone-cold glare, to the two naked people in the room.

"What the hell is going on?" Carmelle shrieks. "Devin?"

"No time for Q and A," Renni says. "Get dressed."

"Holy shidt," the naked lady says, spittle flecking her swelling lip. "You're Rebbi Rabirez."

"And you're deaf," Renni says. "I told you to get dressed."

The naked woman starts to cry, and I feel sick again. Carmelle looks from Renni, to me, and lingers on me. I don't know what to do with this, so I look away. "Come on," she says to her lover, and guides her back into the office, closing the door behind them.

When they're out of sight, Renni immediately falls into action. She helps me into a sitting position, my back propped against the cash register counter. She leaves for a second and comes back with a package of a lingerie nurse's outfit, tearing it open with her teeth.

"This one had the most fabric," she explains as she uses the bra piece to wipe the blood away from my newest wound. "It's not too deep."

She rips pieces of nylon and lace and ties them together, going back for one more package, and ripping and tying, until she's fashioned a bandage for my shoulder which she secures with some pantyhose knotted under my arm pit. Then she fishes inside her pocket and hands me two Endocet.

"You'll have to dry swallow," she says.

For some reason, her saying this reminds me of the giant penis I had been picturing hovering next to her head in Ashbee's, and I start to laugh. I get kind of hysterical as the phantom cock begins to materialize again—this time black, uncircumcised, and unusually veiny. The cock looks less silly with a backdrop of dildos and butt plugs, but it gets too close to Renni's cheek and I pop it with a blink. It spurts and expires like a water bubble.

I swallow the pain pills. "I ruined your dress."

"Haven't you heard?" Renni makes a face like, *meh*. "I'm rich."

We hear some thumping and banging coming from the office, like the sound of rearranging furniture that you learn pretty slowly is probably not what your parents are doing at two in the morning when you can't sleep.

"Hope Carmelle can find her panties," I say. "She loves her panties."

A holdover from her stripping days, her underwear are almost more important to her than her outerwear. She used to love to model them for me. I used to love to test their elasticity with my teeth.

Renni starts sniffing, and scans the ground. "Is this piss?"

I would flush with embarrassment, but honestly I think we're beyond that at this point. Besides: "Zombie," I say.

Renni looks dubious. "Can zombies piss?"

"Zombie!" I shout and point emphatically behind her.

The door to the office opens and Carmelle and her lover—fully clothed now—step out just as Renni leaps up and catches the zombie by its neck as it launches itself into her. Its putrid breath is horrendous from here, but Renni doesn't flinch. It drips unthinkable shit and maggots from its mouth that plop onto Renni's cleavage and slide down. Renni struggles for only a moment, as if to tease the zombie that it might have a chance, then the muscles in her arms tighten, her lips pull back from her teeth, and she slams the zombie's head into the glass countertop, which shatters on impact. Shards rain down on me; I cover my face with my arm, but peek beneath the crook of my elbow to watch Renni slide the axe out of its makeshift sheath on her back, and bring the business end down on the still-twitching zombie's neck. Its severed head rolls to a stop near my feet. Carmelle and her lover shriek in unison.

Then Carmelle notices me. "Devin, oh my God, you're hurt." She squats next to me, tentatively touching my bandages and stroking my hair. Her scent belongs to her lover now, and Carmelle in turn smells like her: cheap cucumber-melon body spray. I don't have the strength to push her away, but apparently I do have the strength to start crying right now, because that is what I start to do.

"Oh, baby," Carmelle croons, crying too. "Baby, what happened to you? What the hell happened?"

Renni comes up behind Carmelle and hoists her up by her armpit—her favorite place to grasp people, evidently. "We'll cover the specifics with you later." She releases Carmelle harshly, then turns to the other woman. "We have to get out of here. More of them will be drawn here by all our noise."

"Whad are dey?" the lover asks.

Renni kicks the severed head in her direction. "What do they look like?"

"Devin needs to get to the hospital," Carmelle says. I'm becoming too familiar with that phrase.

Before everyone can start arguing about what our next move is going to be, I push myself up on shaking arms, palms pressing into glass shards, and make a suggestion.

"Let's get the hell out of this town."

Renni comes over to help steady me, but I hold up my hand, stopping her. "Do you have a car?" I ask the lover. She seems surprised that I'm addressing her.

"Yuh huh," she says with her swollen mouth.

"Give Carmelle your keys." No one questions me. The lover tosses her keys to Carmelle. Everyone looks to me for further instructions. I must look pretty strong and brave underneath all this blood. That, or they pity me. "We'll go to Indiana," I say. "Cherry's there with Brad. We'll call her, meet up, turn on a radio and see how far this thing has spread. After that, if I'm still breathing, we'll go to the hospital. Questions?"

Carmelle goes to touch me again, but I move a little bit away from her. "What do you mean, if you're still breathing?"

Renni wipes off the grime-covered axe blade on the zombie's dust covered back, and sheathes it. "Solid plan, Devin. Twister—" she says, addressing Carmelle, "You go with C-Cup—"

"No," I cut her off. "She rides with you. I'll go with Carmelle."

Renni doesn't fight this decision with anything other than a tendon spasm in her jaw and a minuscule narrowing of her eyes, but it's enough to make me want to explain my reasoning.

"I'm no good on a bike." I rotate my shoulder weakly, wincing. "Can't hold on."

Renni doesn't argue. She throws a sneer at C-Cup. "Might want to tie your hair back. Your head's too big to fit my helmet, and I only got the one." Then she dons her ever-present and miraculously durable sunglasses and heads out over the zombie-strewn threshold.

C-Cup looks one last time at Carmelle—who shoos her along with her eyes—tries not to look at me, and skitters after Renni. Alone with Carmelle, things are quiet. Outside, I hear Renni fire a couple times, the car alarms and dogs continue to sound off, but in here—I can breathe.

Then Carmelle says, "Baby...."

"Is there a back way out of here?" I ask. "We should hurry."

Lover Girl drives a deep maroon Volkswagen Bug, one of the newer, more plastic models, complete with pink fuzzy dice that hang from the rearview mirror and leopard print car seat covers. I do little to hide the pleasure I'm taking in mucking up the decor with all my annoying bleeding.

In the car, Carmelle keys the ignition and says, "Buckle up." I just laugh at her.

It's a little tough getting through Main Street with all its abandoned vehicles clogging the road, but Carmelle manages to get our small car through some tough gaps. It's probably like a video game for her now, like it was for me in the beginning too. A racing game, *Need for Speed* or *Burn Out*, or one of those *Grand Theft Auto* mob capers.

I cough a little bit, and some blood comes out onto my hand. I smear it languidly along the car's freshly waxed dashboard.

Carmelle has decided to take the side streets out of town, which looks to be a good idea. If the crisis is growing, the main throughway will be packed, the highway a nightmare of people who chose "flight" out of their only two survival options. On these side streets, you wouldn't even know there was a crisis, except for how silent it is. Some houses are even boarded up over their windows and doors, as if preparing for a hurricane. Renni keeps pace with us a car length behind, her face masked by the helmet's tinted visor. Carmelle's lover clings desperately to Renni's waist, hair whipping all over her face (guess she couldn't find a hair tie), flicking bugs from her teeth with her tongue.

Carmelle's Lover, C-Cup. I don't want to keep calling her either of these things.

"What's her name?" I ask Carmelle.

She takes a deep breath, like an inverted sigh, and tightens her ten-and-two grip on the steering wheel. "Bambi."

I start to laugh but it quickly morphs into another blood splatter cough, which lasts awhile.

"God, Devin, you're really hurt," Carmelle says.

"Not really."

The Endocet isn't really working, or maybe it is and I'm only feeling a fraction of the pain, but that fraction is pretty high, like a double negative integer, an imaginary number. I don't know. I don't really know math, or metaphors. All I know is I'm tired, and I'm one bite closer to that forever sleep everyone's always writing songs and poems about. It doesn't seem that bad, at this point.

"Oh, baby," Carmelle sobs. Most of her makeup has already sweated off her face, but what little of it remains now drips down her cheeks with her tears. "I never wanted any of this to happen, you know? I never planned any of it. This is the first time we, Bambi and me—it just *happened*." She pauses here, as if waiting for me to argue with her. I slump down lower in my seat and close my eyes. "Baby, I swear," she continues, in that voice she uses when she wants my permission to do something we both know is stupid—*Baby, I swear if we puree these carrots on high we don't have to wait for them to thaw out; Baby, I swear I can stay out until five a.m. and be at work by eight, no problem; Baby, I swear the red light means it's off.* "I swear, baby. It was just this one time. Just this one time."

"Carmelle," I say. "I don't care."

"Don't say that, baby. *Talk* to me."

"We're just roommates anyway," I say, fighting swirls and lines of lasers behind my closed eyes, curiously shaped like zombies. "We were just like roommates. Roommates can't cheat on each other. It's not in their contract."

"How can you say that?" Carmelle's voice rises in direct proportion to her indignation. "We were in love!"

I make a rough choking sound deep in my diaphragm that's meant to be a scoff. "Right. Guess you just never got around to filling me in on that part."

"This isn't my fault!"

I suddenly have this out-of-body experience of floating up near the roof of the car and watching my body move independently of my consciousness. Slowly, my arm reaches out for the door and levers it open, then tucks back into my side, and my whole body, head first, just tumbles right out the door, before Carmelle even has time to slow down. But when I open my eyes, I'm still sitting here.

"This is absurd," I say. "Don't you get it, Carmelle? None of this matters now. Fuck who you want to fuck, love who you want to love. It's all over anyway. That's what all this means." I clutch the bandage on my shoulder, flex the aching muscle in my calf. Briefly, I wonder when the last time was that I got a tetanus shot.

"What if I want to love you?" she asks, in a voice I've never heard from her before—small and uncertain.

I look around behind us at Renni on her motorcycle. I blink back the fuzziness at the edge of my vision. "It might be too late for that."

She thinks I'm still talking about her naughty Twister game with

Bambi. "We can survive this, you know? Haven't you ever heard of couple's therapy? We can get through this. I don't want to lose you."

It's tough not to launch into a barrage of the obvious questions—Then why the fuck did you cheat on me? Blah blah blah blah—but I swallow them down. Because it'd be like asking an unsuccessful suicide victim why they did it, why did they blink at the last second, wince and breathe—"Oh, shit"—and turn their head that fraction of an inch to the left that kept them alive? Who knows, who cares, move on. Move on, move on, move on.

"Everyone makes mistakes," Carmelle says, dodging around a stalled Buick. "I mean, let's face it, we weren't exactly getting along, you and me. We barely see each other anymore. We just don't make the time for each other, like we used to."

"You're right," I say, as dryly as the blood pooling in the back of my throat will allow. "We should make more time. Maybe a game night. I'll go out and buy a deck of cards. You already have Twister."

"I'm being serious, Devin," she says.

"So am I," I say, starting to cough again. "I love Twister."

"Devin," Carmelle starts in, but suddenly we find ourselves merging into heavy traffic on Chester Road—which runs right over the state line—and she slams on the brakes. My body slips forward and my head whiplashes into the dashboard. Just one more bruise to add to my steadily growing collection. No blood, at least, but a head injury is not doing any favors for my fuzzy vision either.

I force myself to focus and look out the windshield at the line of bumper-to-bumper vehicles. Carmelle rolls down her window to get a better view, and a plume of exhaust fumes blows into the car with the warm wind. I can hear horns blaring one after the other, people yelling over the noise for everyone to stop yelling—"Lay off the horn! No one is moving, you get it? You're making it worse, okay!" Chester Road is a four lane throughway running along private farmland, with two lanes heading eastbound deeper into Ohio and two lanes heading westbound to Indiana. But all four lanes are now filled with westbound traffic. We sneak into the fray by virtue of being a compact car, smack in the middle of a white minivan bussing about six kids whose under-ten-years old faces are glued to a DVD playing in the back of one of the headrests, and an F-150 pick up truck loaded with bushels of canned beans, spam, Twinkies, and bottled water. (And, sure enough, a silver set of jumbo-sized truck nuts.)

Renni pulls up to Carmelle's window, and flips up her visor. "I'm gonna ride ahead." She shouts. "Be back."

I have a strange feeling I will never see her again, and my stomach plummets like I've just shot down a roller coaster, but I just nod. Bambi waves stupidly back at Carmelle as they drive away.

"Look, some people are standing on their roofs," Carmelle says, pointing all around us. "We should take a look."

"You go ahead." The effort it would take for me to function my limbs in any other way than I am now—which mainly involves digging my nails into my thighs to keep from crying, and rotating my ankle every now and then to wake up my dead calf—doesn't seem worth it.

"I'll help you," she says. Before I can protest, she's climbed out her side of the car and rounded to mine. The fresh air feels good when she opens the door, but all the noise and the fumes cause me to swoon.

"Easy now," Carmelle says, wrapping her arms around me and lifting me up. That's when I lose it, when all I can feel is her weight on me and my weight on her, and so what if she smells like honeyed almonds or cucumber melon, or coconut, or who the fuck cares. She feels solid, and familiar, and I've missed her so much, and I just want one thing, one thing in the middle of all of this surreal insanity, one thing that's real.

I hold on and cry into her neck, going pretty much limp except for my arms which refuse to let her go. She eases me back into the seat and lets me cry, leaning her thighs against mine, running her fingers over the hair on the back of my neck, whispering into my ear words that don't even make sense to me anymore—"Baby, baby, it's okay, oh baby, my baby, I'm so sorry, everything's okay."

The only thing that breaks us apart is a sound like thunder rolling in from the east. Its effect on the crowd of boisterous traffic is what alarms us into parting—every car horn quiets down, all yellers shut up their mouths, even car engines turn off. Carmelle pulls back just enough for us both to look up out of the open car door and watch the flying V of Air Force jets scream through the sky.

The jets streak by overhead, then pair off and circle to other parts of the city. They're followed by a handful of military helicopters whose jungle camouflage paint only makes them stick out like targets. They fly up a bit further and then break off and hover in circles, flying low. If I squint, I can just make out the silhouette of a gunman seated behind a turret. A Channel Two news helicopter pops out from behind a cloud, but is quickly chased off by one of the military choppers, like a scene out of an absurd Pac Man game.

"Come on," Carmelle turns back to me, lifting me up again. "We have to see what's happening."

I struggle not to wince too much as Carmelle boosts me onto the hood and then to the roof of the car, holding each other as we stare at the scene only a couple hundred yards up from us. Apparently, while we were busy taking the back roads to avoid traffic, our town officials were busy calling in the National Guard to stop it completely. There are several trucks with the National Guard insignia stamped on the sides, some Jeeps, police cars, and four Army caravans crowded together to form a makeshift barricade. There's a swarm of Army men and women and National Guardsmen milling around the barricade, guns held at their sides—big guns, rifles—and some of them are wearing those little white anti-contamination masks.

No one's really doing anything, all of us citizens are just kind of awed, kind of dumbstruck by the whole situation. Sitting back in our cars with our families or friends, just waiting to see what will happen next.

A new caravan of shiny camouflaged trucks and Jeeps pulls up behind the barricade. The front line of vehicles parts slightly to let a big tractor-trailer through; a few people press forward, thinking maybe this is their chance to escape, but some gunmen are on them in nanoseconds, threatening them back. The tractor-trailer rolls forward, and turns left, and we can see what it is hauling: a large concrete wall. A second tractor trailer moves in behind the first and turns right. They set up their perimeter as we watch, dumbfounded. Then some flunkies begin unloading several other trucks, pulling out long coils of crisscrossed wire, bundles of metal poles, and an armload of large posthole diggers. They spread out into the fields at either side of the blocked off throughway, and start laying the fence.

"They're fencing us in," I say. "They're literally fencing us in."

Seeing this, the crowd grows agitated, and they begin their shouts again, this time not calling for people to move their asses but for some sort of explanation. In response, a voice booms out all around us as if being beamed from the clouds.

"Ladies and gentlemen," the voice opens, as if warming up a crowd at a concert hall. "Please return to your vehicles and tune your radios to channel one oh seven point six. Evacuation procedures will be broadcast to you once you have all returned to your vehicles. Ladies and gentlemen, please return to your vehicles and tune your radios to channel one oh seven point six. Evacuation procedures will be broadcast to you once you have all returned to your vehicles. Ladies and gentlemen…."

The voice calls out instructions on a loop, and I look up to see the large box-like speakers hanging over the sides of the circling helicopters, and back at the barricade, where they are also set up in the beds of trucks. There's some complaint among the crowd, but everyone is eager for answers so we all clamber into our cars and tune to the station and wait.

Carmelle shares the passenger seat with me again. It feels comforting to have her next to me, pressed into me, holding me. I want to tell her I forgive her, but I don't know how she'll take it, so I keep my mouth shut.

Finally, after some minutes of static, a very officious male voice crackles over the radio waves and joins us on the Beetle's tinny speakers.

"Citizens," the voice begins, "This is Sergeant Elmer Dunnigan of the National Guard. I will be guiding you through our evacuation procedures. Your bravery and cooperation in this matter is fully expected and appreciated. Do exactly as instructed and we will all make it out of here safe and sound.

"The terrorist situation as of now is at Orange, and we are taking steps to insure it is under control. We plan to evacuate as many of you as possible before quarantine becomes necessary."

"Terrorists?" Carmelle asks. "But they were dead! They were dead, and walking around, and…."

"You really want to hear him say the word 'zombie'?" I ask. "They're trying to keep people calm. 'Terrorist' is less scary. Terrorists they can deal with. Zombies?" I shake my head. "Forget about it."

Carmelle's skin sprouts gooseflesh, and she huddles against me for warmth. "I'm still scared, Devin."

It's my turn to be reassuring, comforting, brave. "We'll make it out of here. Let's just listen to the sarge's plan."

"Officers will be coming around to each vehicle and evaluating you individually for evacuation. Once you pass your evaluation, you will follow the officer to the gate we've set up at the barricade, and they will process you through. Please have all forms of identification ready. We will start with those nearest the barricade and move our way back in waves. Remain in your vehicle until an officer approaches you. Do not exit your vehicle. Remain calm and follow your officer's instructions. This message will repeat.

"Citizens, this is Sergeant Elmer Dunnigan of the National Guard…."

Carmelle reaches out and twists the volume dial down to turn the Sarge's voice to a low background hum, easily tuned out. She rolls the passenger window down and sticks her head out. "We're not too far back," she says back to me. "I can see the officers going up the line, checking IDs." She pushes back into the car and looks at me, smiling. "You're right, we're going to get out of here."

I start to cry again.

"Baby, what is it?" Carmelle puts on her concerned-girlfriend face, the one she's pretty much worn permanently since we started this little road trip, and wraps my head in her arms, hugging me to her face.

"I can't go," I snot into her neck. I'm not sure she's catching any of what I'm saying through the wetness of my speech and how closely I'm speaking into her neck, but I keep talking. "He said they're doing evaluations. Evaluations! They're gonna see I got bit. They won't let me out. I'll be quarantined. Carmelle, don't leave me here, okay? Don't leave me here alone."

"I can't hear anything you're saying," Carmelle says sweetly, and backs my face up. She looks at me and wipes my tears away with her thumbs. All the crying and trying to talk has brought on the coughing fits again and I double over. Carmelle rubs my back until I'm spent.

Finally, I look back up at her, feeling like shit and looking twenty times more terrible, I'm sure. I hold up my hands, stained red with the blood I just coughed into them. "See? I won't pass their evaluations."

Slowly, the realization shadows Carmelle's face, deepening her concerned wrinkles. Her eyes scan my body, lingering over my wounds. She moves her hands as if to lay them over my bandages, but curls her fingers back into her palms and pulls her arms into her chest. She struggles for a minute to come up with something to say, and I struggle to keep down more tears and pleas for her to stay with me. Finally, she says, "Don't tell them."

"What do you mean?"

"Don't tell them what happened. Just tell them...tell them you got trampled in a riot or something. Or.... Wait, see?" She seizes my wrist and holds it up, looping one finger through the loose hospital bracelet I forgot—or never even noticed—I've been wearing. "You were at the hospital, prior to all this shit. Tell them it was a pre-existing circumstance. A dog attacked you. You have evidence. I'll back you up."

Despite how flimsy it is, I am very close to being convinced it will work, dangerously close to the kind of hope that could destroy me. I smile at Carmelle, a hard smile to hold but she deserves it.

"Good idea," I tell her.

She squeezes my snotty, bloody face between her palms and kisses me flush on my snotty, bloody mouth. "I told you, we're gonna get out of here."

"I thought I told you that."

"Then it must be true." She takes my hand and entwines our fingers and holds it in her lap.

With the passenger window still rolled down, we can hear the officers ahead of us, but it's impossible to tell just by sound how far ahead they are. Car doors are slamming, various voices are intoning, babies are crying and kids are screaming, women are crying and men are yelling, but nothing extreme, nothing riotous. So far, it seems everyone is passing their evaluations. Above us, the helicopters circle, gunmen leaning out behind their turrets, and the jets make frequent loops to pass over us higher up. The Sarge drones on in the static of our radio.

"Hey," I nudge Carmelle, nodding at the window. "Can you see if Renni's out there?"

She looks at me for a second like, *Who's Renni?*, then she remembers. She leans out the window and scans the view down the line of cars. She comes back in. "I don't see her, but the officers are only a couple cars up."

Sure enough, two uniformed National Guardsmen approach the driver side and passenger side of the truck in front of us simultaneously. One officer carries a rifle, held in both hands at his stomach, while the other carries a clipboard, and asks the driver of the truck to step out.

"She probably already got out," Carmelle says, petting my arm reassuringly. "She and Bambi are probably already over the state line. I've been meaning to ask you, how did you come to be fighting zombies alongside Renni Ramirez, anyway?"

"Oh, good." I quirk a smile at Carmelle. "You can see her too. I'm not entirely convinced she isn't a hallucination."

"She looked pretty real to me when she was breaking Bambi's nose."

I remember the feeling of Renni's own nose giving out under the force of my misguided elbow. "She's just paying it forward."

"What do you mean?"

"I kind of broke her nose earlier." Carmelle stares at me. "It was an accident."

"She is going to sue you so hard."

"Yeah, well, you can't sue a dead girl."

"Shut up." Carmelle wraps her arms around me and we sit in weighty silence until two officers approach the window.

"Could you step out of the vehicle please, ladies?" The officer who addresses us is young, maybe even as young as me, fresh faced with no traces of five-o'clock shadow or razor burn, hair buzzed at the sides and back to give him a flattop. He wears wire-rimmed glasses and he pushes them up to the bridge of his nose constantly, even though they never slide down. His partner is a woman, slightly overweight but pretty, even with the light blonde mustache she didn't have time to bleach away this morning.

"Can I see some identification please?" Carmelle scrambles in her pockets and pulls out her drivers license. I don't move for mine; I'm looking this kid up and down, trying to evaluate how he's evaluating me. He hasn't even glanced at my wounds once. He keeps his eyes on my face, and on Carmelle's ID when she hands it to him. He copies down her information to his clipboard and hands the license back to her. "And yours, miss?"

Carmelle takes charge, telling them my full name and explaining to the officer that I lost my purse in all the panic, and apologizing for my distant stare. "She's been through so much, even before all this."

"I was attacked by a dog," I blurt out. Carmelle grabs my hand, and pinches it.

"I was in the hospital with her when this all started," she goes on, much more convincing than me. She really is a great actress, a natural. This thought stirs up some bitterness in me and I have to swallow hard to keep it down. "It really freaked us out when we heard about all the terrorist activity. I knew I had to try to get her out of here, to some place safer, a different hospital. The one we were in lost power."

"Saint Mary's?" The female officer asks.

Carmelle brightens at her suggestion. "That's the one," she says.

"My aunt was in there for appendicitis," the female officer goes on. "She barely made it out. Said it got real ugly."

"Oh, well, we must have missed all that," Carmelle says quickly, stroking my arm protectively. "But I'm glad to hear your aunt made it out safely."

"Thank you," the officer says.

The male officer looks our bodies over, starting with Carmelle. "Have you suffered any injuries?"

"Oh, no," Carmelle says, shaking her head. "Like I said, we were in the hospital when all this got going, and we went straight for our car, and then ended up here. We never even saw firsthand anything that's going on. But I won't bother you with questions about any of it; I know you have a job to do."

He seems a bit relieved to hear her say this, but then he turns to me and his brow narrows. "You're injured," he says matter-of-factly.

Again, Carmelle speaks for me. "Yes, she was attacked by our neighbor's dog. A German Shepherd, improperly leashed. Believe me, we will be pressing charges, as soon as things settle down."

"I need to examine the bites, if I may," the officer says, trying to sound stern yet unable to invade my privacy without at least the pretense of my permission.

He starts with my leg, unwrapping the bandage cautiously. The female officer grips her gun a little tighter and discreetly points it at me by angling her body a little to the left so it still appears she's just casually holding it. When the air hits the wound, I wince a little.

"Does it hurt?" The officer asks.

"Like a bitch," I say. I haven't actually looked at the wound since being admitted to the hospital, and I'm too afraid to look now. The officer rewraps the bandage and comes up to undo the one at my shoulder.

He holds up a piece of lacy lingerie. "All out of Ace bandages?"

I can't say anything, and Carmelle just looks distressed. Shit.

He doesn't even unwrap the whole thing, just replaces the lingerie and goes back to jotting things down on his clipboard. He excuses himself for a moment and steps back with the female officer to confer. I watch them pull out a walkie-talkie and talk into it together.

All around us, officers are knocking on windows and leading people pleasantly and professionally to the barricade. The helicopters circling overhead have become just like the wind to me. I look beyond the two officers in front of me, to the barricade, and watch a group of five people in bulky yellow hazmat suits start up the line. Somehow, I know they're coming for me.

"Carmelle," I turn to her. She's crying already. "They're not going to let me through. But they'll let you go. So you should. You should go."

She shakes her head, grabs my hands. "No, no. I won't leave you."

"You don't have a choice," I say. "See those hazmat guys down there? They're coming to quarantine me. They'll probably.... I don't want to think about what they'll probably do to me. But you can't come with me. So, it doesn't really matter, you know? You have to go. I want you to go."

"But, Devin, I...." She can't even finish her sentence, her words are swallowed by her sobs. The two officers are done conferring. The boy with the clipboard turns to us with sorrowful eyes, and the woman levels her rifle at me.

"I'm sorry, Miss Julian," he says to me. "You'll have to follow Officer Briggs. Miss Soufflé? You can follow me."

"Wait," Carmelle says, holding out her arm to ward them off, even though no one has moved toward us and the hazmat guys are still some yards off. "Just fucking wait. Wait. Devin.... I can't believe this."

I hug Carmelle to me, even though the pressure on my shoulder drills up through my bones and needles my brain. I kiss her ear and tell her the thing I've been too afraid to say since the day we met, even though it's the only thing I've wanted to say, the only thing I think that's ever really been true: "I love you."

We cry into each other for a minute, until the young officer coughs politely. Carmelle pulls away from me, pulls away for what I know in my heart to be forever, and goes to follow the young officer, looking back at me the whole way. They pass the hazmat suits, and Carmelle trips one of them, which makes me laugh.

"You don't have to lie anymore," the woman with the rifle pointed at my chest tells me. "You were bitten by one of them, weren't you?"

"Yes," I say. "The terrorists bit me."

"I'm so sorry," she says, sounding genuine, but it's hard to tell with my heart beating so fast, the blood rushing in my ears.

I look at the hazmat team, getting closer. A couple of them have handguns, one of them has handcuffs. "What are they going to do with me?"

Before the officer can respond, I hear the roaring of a familiar engine speeding up from behind me. I turn just in time to almost shit myself as Renni Ramirez screeches to an angled stop mere inches from my ankles. She rips the helmet from her head and shouts at me, "Get on!"

She doesn't have to tell me twice.

The female officer moves her weapon back and forth between us, trying to decide what to do. "Dismount the vehicle!" she screams. Behind her, the hazmat guys have started running.

Without a word, Renni pitches her helmet at the officer. It hits her weapon and she fires, the bullet skimming the asphalt. Mustering up all my strength, I climb onto the bike and cling to Renni's back like she's my last lifeline—which she is. She pivots the bike and takes off down the line of stalled cars, away from the barricade, away from Carmelle, away from safety, and back into the heart of the undead city.

Chapter 6

A MIDSUMMER NIGHT'S DEAD

RENNI RAMIREZ TAKES ME BACK TO HER HOTEL ROOM. Damn, how many lesbians out there wish they could say that? If I live to make it to my ten-year high school reunion, that's all I want my little blurb to say: *Devin Julian, Class of '07, voluntarily taken back to Renni Ramirez's hotel room.* I'd win some kind of silly award, I'm sure.

Unfortunately, the hotel room is pretty much where the fantasy ends. Well, okay, that's not exactly true. Renni Ramirez does tell me to take off my clothes, but it isn't super sexy or anything, considering how bloody and gross and kind of covered in my own urine I am. I'm not even embarrassed to undress in front of her—I think I became immune to embarrassment sometime between elbowing her in the nose and peeing all over her dress. It takes me a little while to get the dress off, because lifting my arms over my head is nearly impossible. Renni helps me slide the spaghetti straps off my arms and pull the dress down over my hips instead, which stretches it out but at this point the dress is a lost cause anyway. I take off my underwear and Renni puts all my clothes into a plastic Kroger shopping bag. She leans into the tub and turns on the hot water.

"I'll find you something to wear," she says, and goes out, closing the door behind her.

We should have gone to a hospital, but we noticed on our way back through the city that some major changes were underway, namely that everyone was getting the fuck out of town. We saw a few pockets of zombies chasing down pedestrians, and Renni stopped when she could to fire off a few bullets into their heads to give the people some more time to escape. Some people decided to loot, as will happen in moments of crisis, so Renni decided to abandon any urban centers. I told her the National Guard woman's story about her aunt barely escaping Saint Mary's hospital, and we both agreed it was safest to stay away, even with the extent of my injuries. Renni told me she was staying at an EconoLodge near the highway, which I thought was kind of ridiculous, but she reminded me of her original plan to keep a low profile. On the way to the hotel, we swung by a pharmacy that Renni had to break into while I sat on the idling bike, white-knuckling her rifle (most of our other weapons were abandoned back at the porn shop, or left in Bambi's car) and looking around me at the barren streets with something bordering on hysteria. Luckily, Renni didn't take too long grabbing up disinfectant, more painkillers, some antibiotics, and proper bandages.

In the bathroom, I reset the water's temperature to cold, because my wounds are already making my whole body hot. I take a moment before stepping into the shower to finally examine my body. My shoulder is the worst, being the freshest. It's stopped bleeding, the blood grown sticky, like a film over Jell-O, and the mouth-sized hole really doesn't look too deep. It's about as round as my fist and there's bruising all around the teeth marks. As for my leg, the nurses stitched it up while I was unconscious and it looks pretty good, some slight bruising, but it's clean. It still throbs painfully and my muscle aches all around it, and this makes my mind go back to tetanus, like maybe I have it. But what can I do about that now? I swipe my bangs away from my sticky forehead and press a pinky finger to my hot skin. There's a bruise forming here too, where my head hit the dashboard, but it's the least of my injuries. All over my arms and feet, I see tiny sparkling bits of glass, but I don't feel them.

In the shower, I savor the cold water as it steams against my skin. It's like burning, in a way, and numbs me somehow, and I'm grateful.

In the closed-in space I can really start to smell myself, and I gag a little. I use almost the entire mini bottle of shampoo and packet of conditioner, scrubbing between my legs and my armpits especially, in case Renni decides to do any more lifting. I'm cautious around the wounds, as they're both tender, especially the shoulder. I pick glass out of my skin and hair and drop it down the drain. When I'm finished, I towel dry, wrap the towel around my body, and step into the main hotel room.

Renni is pulling t-shirts out of her duffel bag and throwing them onto the bed. She stops when I come out. "Feel better?"

"Yeah."

"You smell better."

I go to the bed—the single unmade queen bed that takes up the middle of the room—and lift up a generic black t-shirt. "I could probably fit this one."

Renni swipes it back from me. "Are you crazy? That's my lucky shirt." I can't tell if she's joking. She stuffs the shirt back into her duffel bag. "Here, wear this one."

It's another plain black t-shirt. "Are you sure?" I say, teasing.

Renni ignores me, pulls out a pair of blue jeans and tosses them on the bed. "These might be big on you, but I don't have anything else. We could go out and scavenge again...."

"I'm really tired," I say, feeling the exhaustion more acutely as I give voice to it.

"That's what I thought," Renni says. She rummages through the plastic bags from the pharmacy, pulls out bottles and places them on the table near the window. "Take some of this stuff," she says, clearly very medically inclined. "Don't overdo it. There's a mini-bar under the sink over there, take whatever you want. I'll help you with your bandages when I get back."

"Where are you going?" I ask, fighting back a clingy *don't leave me.*

Renni lifts her duffel bag off the bed and heads for the bathroom. "Shower," she says. "Relax." She touches my arm reassuringly, and disappears into the bathroom.

I hear the shower switch on and try not to picture Renni naked under its stream of water. It's no use; it's all I'm seeing. Then suddenly I'm seeing Carmelle, and then I have to try really hard to push this image out with the image of a giant penis showering, which gives way to an image of Cherry showering, and then I'm back to the image of Renni showering. I can't win.

I take a five-dollar bottle of Evian water from the mini-bar and down a few pills, mostly antibiotics and anti-inflammatories because the pain killers aren't really doing anything so I leave them off the plate. There's some peanuts and almonds and fancy cheese and crackers in the little mini-fridge but I'm not hungry, even though I can't remember the last time I ate, but I think it was some time last night. It's getting into late afternoon and the sun is starting to burn off into its pink haze. I close the curtains and turn on a light instead.

Before putting on Renni's clothes, I bandage up my leg wound, covering it with Neosporin first. Renni's jeans fall loosely over my hips and trail a good six inches over my feet. I roll up the cuffs, and try to tie the rope that used to hold up my weapons around the waist to make a belt, but I can't get it tight enough so I toss the rope aside. I put on the t-shirt and it fits nicely, meaning it must run fairly small on Renni. It's a tight v-neck so it doesn't show anything off, but it's pretty obvious I'm not wearing a bra. The cotton fabric scratches against my shoulder wound, and I remember I was supposed to wait for Renni to bandage it, so I take off the shirt and wrap the towel back around my chest when Renni steps out of the bathroom.

She got dressed inside the bathroom and now wears a pair of sleek red basketball shorts and what I can only assume is her lucky black t-shirt. I was right, it does fit her snugly, and I have to look away to keep from staring. Her hair is still wet and kind of curly now, sticking to her neck a little. She smells good, like the motel's shampoo but also like something else, something…good. I don't know. Is it getting hot in here?

She drops her duffel bag against a wall, grabs a water from the mini-bar, and joins me on the bed. I sit against the headboard with my legs out, my injured calf propped up on a pillow because all I remember from Girl Scouts is you're supposed to keep sprained ankles elevated and this comes close enough. Renni sits cross-legged at my side—man, what gorgeous legs, so close to mine—and starts going through the medical supplies I laid out on the bed next to me.

"This is gonna sting," she says, and pours some iodine out onto a washcloth and dabs it against my shoulder wound. I wince a little but really the pain is nothing compared to the bite that created the need for it. She applies a bandage and wraps it up with expert fingers. "You take some of these?" She shakes the bottle of antibiotics, and I nod.

Renni gathers everything up and puts it back on the table. "You should eat something."

"I'm not hungry." Besides, sitting here on this bed feels so good, I can't imagine ever standing up again.

"Then you should sleep," she says.

"Yeah," I say. "That will probably happen." I feel my eyes getting heavy, my whole body getting heavy, but I fight it, because I just thought of something else and I have to know. "Renni," I say, only the second time I've said her name. She looks at me. "Why did you come back?"

"They wouldn't let me leave," she says, and runs her finger over the severely shallow cuts on her arms, more like minor scrapes she could have picked up from falling into a rosebush or something. "Not taking any chances. Probably wanted to quarantine me too, but I bailed. That other chick made it out though."

"But you came back for me."

She shrugs and sits down at the table, takes a drink of water. "I don't know anyone else in Ohio."

"Oh," I say, and pinch my eyes with my thumb and forefinger. My headache is renewing itself.

"That not what you wanted to hear?"

"What? No. Yeah. It's fine." I remember her question to me in the hospital, asking me if I wanted her to leave. She's not asking now.

"Shit's gone crazy," she says. "I'm not really sure what I'm doing. Are you?"

"I'm pretty much dying," I say, not trying to be dramatic, but there it is. "Or turning into a zombie."

"Quit with that zombie shit," she says, taking another drink, pulling from the plastic sixteen-ounce bottle as if it were a fifth of Jack Daniels. "If it was gonna happen, it would have happened by now."

"Maybe," I say. "But you might want to book a separate room for yourself, just to be safe."

Renni sets her water on the table, gets up and comes over to the bed. She presses her palms to the headboard at either side of me and leans her face close enough to mine that I can smell her freshly brushed teeth (spearmint toothpaste, the best kind).

"I'm not scared," she says.

This next moment is either the biggest mistake of my life, or the greatest moment I'll ever experience, but I don't let myself dwell on the hypothetical duality of this moment's nature, I just do it, because it feels, if not exactly right, at least necessary, inevitable.

I tilt my chin up an inch to meet hers and I kiss her. I just plant one on her, the same way Carmelle planted one on me over a year ago. And Renni, she does this amazing thing: she closes her eyes. Our lips are pressing together and then parting slightly and pressing again, tongues just beginning to enter the equation, when I figure I should be polite and also close my eyes. And this is when I realize I couldn't possibly have made the biggest mistake of my life by kissing Renni, because that honor will have to go to having just closed my eyes. Because immediately the room spins, the bed swooshes out from under me and I'm falling, even though I can still feel her lips on mine, and I know I have to open my eyes but they're too heavy and I can't do it, and then my stomach drops out, my throat swells up, I feel something pushing, crawling, gasping to be released, and I can't hold it down, the pressure builds and builds and builds, and I have to let go.

My eyes open as I vomit into Renni Ramirez's mouth.

There isn't even a sound to warn her, it just comes out slick and silent, a pinkish white liquid that is comprised of mostly bile, I'm guessing, as I haven't eaten anything in over eighteen hours. It splashes onto her bottom lip and her eyes fly open and she jerks her head back.

"Mother of shit!" she says, spitting onto the floor, and then she's doubled over and vomiting herself.

I grab my mouth with my hand and run to the bathroom, because there's still vomit dripping between my fingers and more on the way. I make my deposit into the toilet, flush it down, and then just sit there. I can't even cry anymore, even though I desperately want to, but my body just doesn't have anything left to give. I rest my head on the lip of the toilet bowl and close my eyes, and feel my consciousness carried off by the weight of the day.

I'm woken up sometime later by the sound of a large insect buzzing against the end table. I peel my eyelids back just enough to blurrily make out a dark, boxlike shape on the table next to my head.

Not an insect, my phone. It's on vibrate, and someone is calling me. *Carmelle,* I think, and reach for the phone.

Bad idea. I'm lying on my stomach, so I reach out with my right arm, the uninjured arm, but the movement still pulls along my shoulders and sends the pain stab-stab-stabbing through me again. It's a ripple effect that jolts my whole body awake, and I gasp a little at the suddenness of it. Then the phone is in my hand and I've pressed the talk button.

"Ugh," I say, meaning hello.

"Devin, you're still alive!" It's Cherry's voice on the other end, sounding annoyingly jubilant. "At least, I think you are. Are you?"

"Cherry?" My voice comes out kind of scratchy, kind of deeper than usual, almost sexily husky. "Where are you?"

"Yay! You are alive!" I hear her clapping on the other end, and then a loud staticky clatter. A second later she comes back on the line, laughing. "Sorry, I dropped the phone. Where are you?"

"I'm still in the city. Isn't Carmelle with you?"

"No, I thought she was with you," Cherry says. "What do you mean you're still in the city? The news said they evacuated everybody. That's why I'm calling, to meet up."

"I'm afraid that's not possible." The bed shifts next to me and I crane my neck around a little—stabby pain stabbing again—to see Renni roll over on her side so that her closed eyes face me. She still looks asleep. I lower my voice to a whisper. "I've been bitten, so they wouldn't let me out. But Carmelle should be in Indiana. She was supposed to find you. Give her a call."

"I will, but Devin, no, you can't stay there." Cherry's annoyingly chipper vibrato becomes alarmingly...alarmed.

"I can't leave yet," I say. "They want to quarantine me. God knows what that means."

"But Devin, they're moving into the city, all the military guys, with guns, and...and...and...."

"What, Cherry?"

"...They have orders to shoot anything that moves! We saw it on the news. Oh God, Devin, please get out of there. They said it, they said they're not looking for survivors because anyone left in the city will already be infected by the nerve gas—"

"Gas?"

"—Yeah, gas, the terrorist bullshit, you know? They said they'd already be infected and they can't risk the spread of infection. They said they'll continue broadcasting the evacuation procedures until six a.m., but then the whole city's getting quarantined, and they're sending in soldiers to burn out the infection. Meaning, I guess, you."

I swallow hard. My phone starts to beep at regular intervals, meaning my battery is about to die. "Cherry, what time is it now?"

"A little before midnight," she says. "We just watched the special report on the eleven o'clock news. Go to an evacuation station, Devin, they're all over the major streets out of town. Let someone know you're alive."

Renni's knee juts into my hip as she tosses and turns again. "No," I tell Cherry. "If they're coming in here ready to kill anything that moves, what do you think they'll do to me if I show up, admitting to having been bitten by two zombies?"

"Two?"

"It's been a long day."

"I don't think they'd hurt you, Devin, I really don't. Maybe they would if…if…."

"If I started changing?"

"But they won't if you look fine."

I'm not sure how I look, but I sure do feel like shit, kind of a running theme. Sleep did help clear my head a little though; a lot of the pressure has dissipated, and my vision has cleared up, the constant throbbing in my head died down a little. My phone beeps into my ear. "I have to go, Cherry. Phone's dying. Call Carmelle, make sure she's safe, okay?"

"Okay, Devin, but—"

"We'll figure something out."

"We?"

The phone shuts down, and I drop it back onto the end table. Cautiously, but with a fair amount of wincing despite this, I roll over onto my back, and turn my head to look at Renni. She's lying on her back now too, one arm splayed out to the side, the other curled against her stomach. Her hair is strewn across her cheek, hiding her face from me, and I want to move it but I don't. Her left knee still juts out far enough to touch my own leg, her other leg sticking straight out in her basketball shorts. I listen to the soft sounds of her breathing, and try to think about what to do next, but watching her sleep is the best plan I can come up with, so that's what I do.

The room doesn't smell like vomit, so I figure she must have cleaned it up. There are some dark stains on the carpet leading to the bathroom. I smack my lips together and taste the inside of my mouth, which tastes vaguely like spearmint toothpaste. I notice she dressed me in her black t-shirt before tucking me into bed. She's saved my life more than once today, and all I've done is break her nose and thrown up in her mouth. She's taken such good care of me, when I've done nothing to deserve it. Unfortunately, I need her to carry me just a little bit farther.

I reach out and shake her shoulder a little. "Renni, Renni. Get up."

She struggles against waking, throwing her head from side to side. "Five more minutes," she mumbles, like a reluctant school child.

"No can do," I say, still shaking her. "We need all the minutes."

She shoots her right arm across her body and grabs my wrist, twisting as she lifts up and slams my body back on the bed. I cry out, and she releases me, then her eyes open. "Oh shit, I'm sorry."

I hold my poor wrist to my chest and rub down the soreness. "No problem."

"Shit, I wasn't even awake." Her eyes glisten in the dark and her forehead creases in concern. It's cute.

"Master reflexes," I say, trying to smile so she'll see I'm okay.

"You're good?"

"I'm good."

She punches me playfully in the ribcage. "What the hell'd you wake me up for?"

I sit up. "Bad news. What else?"

"Let me pee before you give it to me," she says, leaping off the bed like it's Christmas morning. I guess the sleep helped her energy level too.

While she's in the bathroom, I hobble over to the mini bar, stretching out my legs. My back cracks a little, but I enjoy it, it means I'm alive. Still alive, not dead, or undead. This infection is taking forever. Unless I'm immune. Could I really be that lucky? I have Renni Ramirez as my guardian angel, and now my blood is immune to the zombie virus. I just can't let myself believe it.

When Renni gets out of the bathroom, I have a smorgasbord of cheese and crackers and mixed nuts and chocolate candies waiting for her on the bed. We eat it all as I go over the news Cherry shared with me, letting the sounds of our chewing fill the gaps of silence where both of us try and fail to come up with a suitable plan.

"There has to be a way out that the brass hasn't thought to block off," Renni says, stuffing a handful of ten-dollar Ritz crackers into her mouth. "It's your town," she says with her mouth full. "Got any ideas?"

I do have one idea, but it involves staying here in this hotel room, naked and together under the covers, sharing a beautiful thing with each other until the gunmen knock our door down at six a.m. There are worse ways to go.

"I don't know," I say, picking the skin off a peanut. "We could try to sneak over the fences they've made. Unless they have guards linking arms across the entire perimeter, there's gotta be unprotected gaps we could sneak through."

"That's risky," Renni says, pinching her bottom lip with her fingers as she thinks. "Zombies I can handle; they don't have guns. Bullets are harder to fight against, that's why I'm usually fighting *with* them."

"You could still go," I say. "They'd let you out."

"If you remind me that I can go one more time, I will," she says, eying me under inscrutable eyebrows. I don't say anything, preferring instead to play with the fringe on my pillow.

Renni redirects back to the subject at hand. "Is there like a, a lake or river or something that they wouldn't think to block?"

I shake my head. "No. This county is pretty dry."

"What about like, the sewers? Or—"

I nearly jump up off the bed, startling our empty paper plates and snack cartons onto the carpet. "That's it! Not sewers—'cause ew, gross—but tunnels. You remember like ten years ago when there was that whole trenchcoat mafia thing scaring the shit out of suburban schools?"

"Sure."

"Well, my high school took measures in case of attack. They planned out these elaborate escape tunnels that go straight to the police station, the hospital, and—guess where else?"

"Indiana?"

"Indiana! 'Cause that's where the nearest SWAT-team unit would assemble, should they become necessary."

"And these tunnels are just running all over beneath this town?"

"Yep. We can get to them from my high school; it's closer to us here than either the hospital or the police station, plus I don't know where to find the tunnels at those locations. But the school's tunnels start in the basement, near the boiler room. I know right where it is."

"Wait, so, your school had these tunnels built to safely evacuate students in the event that some kid went homicidal and started shooting his classmates, right?"

"That was the idea. They never got any use, though. Thankfully."

"But everyone knew about them. You'd just post a guy at the entrance to the tunnels and take out rows of kids lining up to evacuate like it was a fire drill."

"Look, I didn't say it was a good plan. But hey, tunnels! We can get out!"

"All right," Renni says, slapping her thighs for emphasis. "Let's load up."

Renni still has her rifle, her axe, a couple handguns, two hunting knives, and loads and loads of ammo. Now that I'm wearing pants as opposed to a dress, I can stash a handgun in one pocket and two extra magazines in the other, and clip the knife to a back pocket. Renni retires the axe from her back, slings the strap of the rifle over her shoulder, and pockets extra ammo and the second handgun and knife. She's changed back into her camo pants, still in her lucky black shirt. She also had an extra pair of sneakers in her duffel bag, which fit surprisingly well on me. We each pop a couple of painkillers and head outside, this hotel room—and everything that happened inside—soon to be forgotten.

We quickly realize that taking Renni's motorcycle to the school is not an option. The streets are crawling with zombies. Should I say shuffling with zombies? Although a few of them that don't have legs are actually crawling, pulling themselves forward with their elbows. Anyway, there are a lot of them roving around, pretty scattered, so I'm guessing not on the hunt. We observe them from the second floor of the hotel for a few minutes; they seem fairly aimless. They run into still objects, into each other, and just bounce off, maybe moaning awkwardly, and turn around and try out a new direction. It'd be comical if my shoulder and right calf didn't throb with the reminder of what these things are capable of.

Without saying anything, Renni and me just look at each other to confirm what we both know: no bike. It would make too much noise and draw their attention. It's time to switch into stealth mode.

Renni takes the lead down the stairs, which apparently lethargic zombies have a difficult time climbing as we encounter no surprises on the way down. In the parking lot, we duck behind cars and scuttle along as quickly as possible. My knife clatters to the pavement once, and I wince, but I manage to pick it up and shove it back into my pants without arousing any zombie interest.

Once we make it out of the parking lot and onto the streets, it becomes increasingly easier to avoid the zombies. They all seem to be heading in the same direction, toward the center of town, where I imagine they are drawn by the residual scent of all those humans—otherwise known as fresh meat—who recently swarmed there, waiting for evacuation instructions. Renni falls back and lets me take the lead, and I take her down a couple side streets, where it's so quiet you can hear the hum of people's refrigerators inside their abandoned houses, and then onto a little dirt road shortcut that zigzags into someone's multi-acre farmland, where the full bright white light of the moon shows us there are no zombies for hundreds and hundreds of yards.

I point into the darkened distance. "There's a hill just beyond those trees on this side of the silo, see it? We pass over that and cross a cow pasture, then there's the Baptist church, and we can cut across Old Mill Road to take us back to Lineman Street, which hooks up with Delaware, which is where the high school is. It's kind of an indirect route, but it seems safer, don't you think?"

Renni shrugs and trudges along behind me. "You're the boss."

As we walk in silence, trying not to dwell on how much time we have left before more things try to kill us (T minus four hours and fifty-six minutes), I think about what it will be like to see my high school again. Even though I still live in the same town, I haven't been back to the school since I graduated four years ago. I didn't think I'd go back until my ten-year reunion, and even then I had a long list of stipulations that my life had to live up to before I would go back for that either (for example, I would be married or at least allowed to be married and have a longterm partner, I would have traveled to at least three different countries, and I'd have either a bachelor's degree in something that sounded impressive or a job title that sounded even more impressive, and that's just for starters). It's not that I had the worst time ever in high school, it's just that I did exactly two things in high school, which probably had a strong correlation to each other: I ate my feelings, and I never got laid. I had a great group of friends, none of whom knew I was gay and all of whom I haven't spoken to in three years, and I stayed under the radar of most bullies. But I was a different person then, completely. Now look at me, I have my own place (a four-hundred-square-foot studio apartment above a decrepit pet store that's probably actually a meth lab), a longterm partner (who has at least one of her own partners, but I've forgiven her for that), a recent promotion within a promising and financially stable company (an outlet furniture store, but everyone flubs their résumés), and while I haven't been to any other countries (or any other towns), it has only been four years and who knows what the next six will bring?

Okay, trying to stay upbeat about this is really not working. Maybe I'll turn into a zombie by then, and show up all cracked out on my own insatiable need to feed, and bring down a couple of the former jocks and chicks who got pregnant and dropped out early to get their GEDs. Or maybe I'll end up with some awesome blood abnormality that produces a natural cure to zombification and I'll reverse all the zombies into people again (though then they'll still be dead, but still, lesser of two evils here) and I'll be this like local folk hero and someone will write a song about me. And then I'll roll into the old cafeteria with Renni Ramirez draped over my arm and we'll sip wine coolers and regale all my former classmates-cum-superfans with the story about our disastrous first kiss.

I'm pulled from this delightful reverie by a sudden chill that brings with it an annoying moisture. I hold out my hand like the rest of me isn't exposed and wriggle my fingers in the rapidly falling droplets.

"Fuck," Renni says, looking up at the gray clouds moving through the dark black sky. "I just washed my hair."

I laugh a little, kind of one of those polite laughs I usually reserve for customers who think they're funny—"I need another chaise longue like I need a hole in the head, har har."—but for some reason it just keeps going, I just keep laughing, and then I'm laughing because of how absurd it is that I keep laughing, and the cycle renews itself.

Finally, Renni grabs my wrist, slick with the falling rain, and jerks me to attention. "What the hell's wrong with you?" She doesn't say it mean, though, but kind of like she finds it amusing.

"You're funny," I tell her.

"Of course I'm funny," she says. "My acting coach told me I had a real sense for comedic timing. Hey." She holds my wrist closer to her face. "You have a tattoo?"

"Oh yeah, it's an emotional beet." We've stopped walking at this point, about halfway up the hill. The moon is brighter here, despite the clouds rolling through and breaking open on us. It bathes Renni's skin in a pale light that makes her look like she is glowing.

"An emotional beet, huh?"

"Yeah," I take my wrist back and massage the tattoo. "Carmelle thought it was funny."

Renni blows air out of her nose that steams in the rain, and looks away.

"What?" I ask her, curious about her sudden rigidity.

"Nothing," she says, in a tone that insists it's something.

"You don't like Carmelle? To be fair, you didn't really properly meet her."

Renni turns back around, eyes wide, and presses her hand to her chest. "*I* didn't properly meet her? Me? What about you? Have you met her? Because I think you got it backwards. I met her in that porn shop back there, and you refuse to."

"Okay, whatever," I say, starting back up the hill.

"Yeah, whatever," Renni says, following me. "Whatever princess wants, princess gets, even if it's your dignity."

I spin around at her, surprised at my own vehemence. "What the hell are you even talking about?"

"I'm talking about how you let that bitch walk—"

"—don't call her that."

"—all over you. You let her fuck someone else right in front of you and then you just walk it off, like maybe she just fucking slipped."

"You don't know what you're talking about," I say, spit and rain flying off my lips as my voice rises. "You don't even know Carmelle, or me, or anything about us."

"Sure, you're right, I don't know you. So tell me then. Tell me you don't let her do whatever she wants without explanation, even when it hurts you. Tell me you don't bend over and take it."

"Fuck you," I yell, and push her. She slides down the hill a little bit, the earth having gone soft under the rain's pelting, but comes back at me, getting closer.

"Yeah, yeah, fuck me, great. Fuck you, and fuck her. She's leading you around by your goddamn clit and you're just pleased as fucking daisies to follow her."

"What the hell happened to you that you're projecting all your shit onto me?"

"Projecting? I'm just observing."

"Some guy must have really dicked you over good—"

"This isn't about me—"

"—for you to come on this strong—"

"—this is about your bitch girlfriend—"

"—lecturing me about a situation where you know nothing—"

"—and her naked friend, shitting all over you—"

"—no one is shitting on me!"

"—and when this is all over, you're gonna go back to her and say, please, please, Carmelle, shit on me some more, I fucking love it!"

"And what the hell are you gonna do, huh? What loser piece of shit are you gonna go back to? The guy who ditched you on your cross-country tour? Or some other Hollywood shit bag?"

"Oh, why do you care?"

"Why do *you* care?" I throw my hands up, rain sloshing off my arms. Renni is inches from me again, and I feel the urge to push her again, but I don't. I just scream louder. "What the hell business is it of yours?"

"What, you think I can't care about you, or any of this crazy shit that's going down here? You think I'm just Renni Fucking Ramirez, hitting a snag, a little inconvenient snafu, on my fucking million-dollar vacation to Buttfuck, Ohio?"

"Yeah, that is what I think, sure. You *are* just Renni Fucking Ramirez, you don't care—"

"—I don't care?"

"—You don't care—"

Her face comes at mine so hard our foreheads crunch together before our lips do. Her mouth suction-cups to mine and the only thing I can do to keep standing up is to press my mouth into hers. Her tongue gropes around inside my mouth, searching for my throat, battling against my own tongue, which darts and parries and generally enjoys itself. She buries her fingers in the neck of my t-shirt and holds me to her, swallowing my face, and I have little choice but to wrap my arms around her head and follow suit. This isn't some wimpy half-assed trial kiss extended hesitantly on a cheap hotel mattress seconds before exhaustion, blood loss, and uncertainty come bubbling up through your stomach and spill out all over the already awkward moment. No, no. This is a raw, primal, desperate kiss, a life-and-death kiss, a hang-on-tight-'cause-this-ride's-just-getting-started kiss.

We push our bodies into each other, until the physicality and heat of our grappling overwhelms our sense of the wider world, which spits rain down on us like a drooling god and harbors demons in its soggy shadows. I don't feel anything other than her mouth—her pressing lips, her licking tongue, her smooth chin that bobs and juts against my own. At one point, I know I knock against her nose with my own and it hurts her—she makes a yelping sound in the back of her throat—but it doesn't stop her; in fact, she presses into me harder. I can't tell if the wetness on and around my mouth comes from her saliva or from the rain.

Eventually, she overpowers me in our erotic struggle, and my heels slip on the increasingly muddy grass, and I go down, slamming hard on my tailbone. My fall pulls us apart for a fraction of a second; I don't even open my eyes. Renni is on top of me, kissing me just as forcefully as if there had been no interruption. She spreads her legs around mine, straddling my thighs, and the heat of her lower half on mine ignites me. I pull at her shirt, jostling the equipment she still has strapped to her back by her makeshift belt. Wordlessly, she breaks apart from me briefly to slip the thing off over her head and then she's back on top, pressing me into the soft, wet earth.

We grope around like this for a long time. At least, I think it's a long time. We've entered some kind of angry, sexy vortex where time, much like the physical world, does not exist. When I start to feel the mud gripping onto my elbows, I just adjust my position so my arms are wrapped around Renni, my fingers buried in her hair, or pawing at her breasts underneath her shirt. When the wetness of the grass seeps into the butt of my pants, I just thrust my pelvis up into Renni's thigh and concentrate on the heat there. She pulls at my hair and sucks at my face and rolls me around and I'm sure she doesn't feel anything outside of me either.

The painkillers are doing their job, numbing the impact all this jostling should have on my poor shoulder and weak calf. My blood surges with adrenaline, and in a fit of inspiration I maneuver my legs around Renni's waist and push up from the ground, rolling her onto her back. I grind myself into her, and I open my eyes and look at her, her wet hair splayed about her face, rain stinging her cheeks, which have flushed red with all this effort. She opens her eyes too, and suddenly we're seeing each other, and I'm afraid for a second that this will break the spell, but then her hand slips underneath the loose waistband of my jeans and I stop worrying.

It's about this time that I notice some movement near the tree line at the bottom of the hill. I glance up, peering out under my dripping brow, and watch a small group of zombies—maybe six or seven—slither out of the forest like upright tree slugs. They're ambling, the way zombies do, and they're quite a distance away from us; maybe two hundred yards.

Renni's fingers have found their way inside me and I gasp and look back down at her. She hasn't noticed the zombies. She stares at me intently, breathing through her mouth as she works inside my pants, and I'm sure my face twists and contorts with each new trick she tries. I look back up to the zombies, who haven't advanced much. Renni grabs my hair with her free hand and lifts herself up, so that she can attach her mouth to my neck. The dual sensations at either end of my body send spasms rippling up my spine. I make some kind of wet, surprised sound, and my eyes flutter closed, my body goes rigid, all the heat bursts away from me, out of every pore, every crack and cranny in my skin, and then I relax.

Renni retracts her hand. She presses both palms to either side of my face and kisses me, a different kind of kiss, a softer, graceful kind, but still with a little tongue. I try to return the kiss, but suddenly I am cold all over, as the world comes rushing back to me—the rain, the wind, the mud, the moaning, the scrape-slosh-scraping—and my wounds begin to throb.

I break apart from her, not very kindly, and look back to check on my pack of zombies. They're about a hundred yards away now, and seem to be quickening their pace (as much as their brittle and broken legs will allow), heading right for us, releasing their low, ghostly moans of anticipation. Renni tilts her head back and sees what I see; I feel her body tense up beneath me.

That's when I hear it fully, the scrape-slosh-scraping, that couldn't possibly be coming from this pack of zombies a football field length away. The rain makes it harder to triangulate the position, but my heart catches in my throat, my bowels churn deep inside me, and I roll off Renni just in time to see we are surrounded.

They come from the top of the hill, sliding down impossibly fast; they come from the left and from the right of the hill, the mud tripping them up here and there, but mostly helping them along with its slick, rapid surface. Before I can even push myself to my feet, the moon is eclipsed by a trio of twisting, dripping bodies, and my ears are plugged with the sound of their moans like screeching.

"Renni!" I scream, and clutch at her slippery hand. Then the undead bodies fall on us, enshrouding us. And the rest is silence.

Chapter 7

And You Will Know Us by Our Trail of Undead

Okay, I lied; the rest isn't exactly silence (I stole that line from a bad '90s movie, or maybe Shakespeare) so much as it is a cacophony of noises that all become one, deafening noise: the sound of me screaming.

The things that I see happening all around us—after the zombies fall away from me, parts of their heads and brains blowing into my face, getting caught in my teeth, my nose, the corners of my squinting eyes—must surely be emitting some type of sound, but like I said, me screaming. Here are the things I see, all at once, but ordered here for a clarity I don't possess in the field:

A. As stated, a zombie's face blown apart by a soundless bullet.

B. A zombie, fresh hole in its head, falling onto Renni as another behind it explodes from the neck up, and falls, decapitated, onto the first zombie. Renni twists beneath them, mouth forming angry words, but she's pinned.

C. The band of zombies that encircles us silently taking a knee as if in prayer, as pieces of their heads and faces plop onto the soggy ground. Lights jump behind them, casting them into silhouetted relief, which makes them slightly more horrifying as the more or less intact ones continue to advance.

D. A squad of dirt bikes cresting the hill, the people onboard masked by their helmets, swinging baseball bats and tire irons and shower-curtain rods at any still-moving face. Behind these, a Jeep with spotlights, spitting up mud from its roiling tires, the shadows of two or three people leaning out over its open top, firing off rifles at their undead targets.

The bikes circle tightly around Renni and me, still lying, shocked or trapped, on the ground. Even though they kick up more mud on us, I'm overwhelmingly grateful for their presence; they rescued us. Their tight circle forms a protective seal around us, and they stop, kicking out legs to lean on while they brandish their mêlée weapons, and stare out at the dropped zombies, not taking any chances. The Jeep takes a couple laps around them, rolling over zombie flesh and bones with no qualms, popping off a shot here and there, until finally, this vehicle also stops.

As the spotlights on the Jeep click off, I can hear again. I've stopped screaming. The dirt-bike engines rumble reassuringly, and people's muffled voices shout beneath their helmets. A couple of people jump down from the Jeep and approach the circle. Immediately to my right, Renni punches one of the dead zombies in the face, and shouts, "Get this fucker off of me!"

Finally able to move again, I spring into action (momentarily inspecting my pants to make sure they are soaked through from the still-falling rain and not my overactive bladder), bolting up and lugging the second zombie off of Renni. She kicks the other one to the side and fumbles to get up. I grip her forearm and pull, and she grips my good shoulder for leverage. Two of the dirt bikes part like a gate and a dark, imposing figure steps into our inner circle.

He stands at a little over six feet tall, deep black shirt clinging to his barrel chest, the short sleeves frayed at the ends as if his muscles flexed one too many times and tore them apart. He wears black militia-style cargo pants and shin-high black lace-up combat boots, similar to Renni's, but heavier looking. Crisscrossed over his chest is a double strand of extra silver-tipped rifle rounds. His rifle casually rests over his shoulder, his finger comfortably planted against the trigger, his other hand reaching to his bearded mouth to remove the stub of a soggy, unlit cigar. His short black hair is matted to his large forehead, and the straps of his eyepatch disappear into its scraggly depths. He's like a more pissed off Nick Fury, crossed with a calmer, taller Wolverine.

"You ladies lost?" he shouts over the rain. His one exposed eye glints at us and he sneers a little.

I'm kind of at a loss for words. On the one hand, he and his people just rescued me and Renni from an ugly death, one I'm not sure even Renni's physical cunning and action-girl strength could have gotten us out of. But on the other hand, he is kind of scary and I don't know what he wants.

"What do you want?" Renni just up and asks him. Subtly, and probably not even consciously aware of it, she has straightened up to her full height and circled in front of me, her arms held out protectively at her sides, blocking my body from this guy's view. She's instinctively protecting me, which makes me feel simultaneously proud but small, like she thinks in some ways I am still a kid.

The man laughs boisterously. "Well, that's a fine how-do-you-do!" Renni lets him laugh through her silence. Some of the people on their dirt bikes turn around to watch us, but he doesn't look at them. Finally, he sticks the cigar back into the corner of his large mouth, and speaks through it, "Come with me if you don't want to get dead."

"Where?" Renni demands.

The man cocks his head in the direction over the hill. "Fullmont High School. Base camp. Impenetrable. You ladies can make me dinner. As a thank you."

He doesn't wait for a response, just turns around and heads back to his Jeep.

Renni looks at me. I nod at her, confirming that the location of his base camp is also our destination. She nods back, silently agreeing to go with him. She stoops to pick up her dropped axe and rifle, and we follow the guy back to his Jeep.

We climb into the backseat beside a skinny boy dressed all in black. He wears a black beret and handles his hunting rifle like it's a third arm; slightly awkward, but also natural. He looks incredibly young in the blue tint of the moonlight, the rain washing over the smooth skin of his cheeks. He doesn't look at either Renni or me but keeps his eyes trained on the edge of the tree line. Up front, the Nick Fury guy takes his seat behind the wheel and pops the clutch, throwing the Jeep into gear and peeling backwards out of the mud. A second man sits in the passenger side, ageless because I can only see the back of his dark, buzzed head. He points his rifle off into the distant fields and his body rocks with every bump and jolt the Jeep takes.

I'm sitting between the young gunman and Renni in the back, so that I have nothing to hold onto as we careen past the dirt bikers, who kickstart their engines to follow us, and lightly lift off from the earth as we shoot over the lip of the hill. I bounce a good six inches off the seat and yelp. I dig my fingers into the padded seat when I come back down, and catch Renni laughing raucously at me out of the corner of my eye. She, of course, has the frame of the Jeep to hold onto. Lucky bitch.

Nick Fury and his lackeys keep silent as we ride along the fields, finally crossing onto the side streets I intended to walk us through, passing the church, the general store, moving into residential territory, then there it is in the distance, the two-story brick building that held my life in suspension for four whole years. The wind picks up as we near it, as if warding us off, and in the distance thunder claps violently and lightning splits the sky. In the tail of its luminescent burst, I can see the dark outlines of a few scattered zombies, lumbering down alleyways, crawling out of the shadows between cars abandoned on the street.

Nick Fury turns wide with one hand, lifting at least two of our four tires off the asphalt, and squawks into the CB radio attached to the dashboard of the jeep: "McMillan, Harm's Way, coming through."

It's almost like a code, until I read by the faded orange light of the street lamps that flicker quickly by, the words "Harm's Way" etched into the dash above the radio dials. It must be the name of the guy's Jeep. Pretty clever, I have to admit. "Get out of Harm's Way." Yeah, I like it.

"Roger that," comes the response on the radio. "South entrance," it says, and Nick Fury makes another one-armed, wild turn. I begin to feel queasy.

We shoot through the parking lot, parallel to the darkened building. At first it looks like all the lights are off, nobody home, but I squint and think I see why: all the windows on the ground floor have been covered by opaque plastic sheeting or planks of wood. Perhaps the lights attract the zombies, and the people inside are trying to pretend like no one is home. But if that's the case, we sure are behaving counterintuitively, revving our engines seven strong through this parking lot, headlights blazing.

The Jeep pulls up close to the double-wide doors leading to the gymnasium, and the doors open only once our bumper nearly grazes them. Light and heat emanate forth from the depths of the gym and we drive, a little slower now, right into it. The dirt bikes take up our rear, and the doors are closed by two large men, probably basketball players, who wrap a heavy chain around their handles, securing them behind us.

Fury kills the engine, flicks his cigar at a kid who has suddenly appeared at his door holding up a blue bucket. The soggy cigar stub plunks into the plastic bucket, a small amount of water spraying up as the cigar hits bottom. The kid can't be older then ten, maybe eleven, and he's scrawny, his twig arms poking out of his horizontally striped Abercrombie and Fitch polo shirt like popsicle sticks on a homemade Christmas ornament. He smiles wide at the large militia leader, as if he is in awe. Fury climbs out of the Jeep and ruffles the kid's hair, then moves on without a word. The kid shuffles after him.

Our two other companions jump down out of the Jeep and we think it's best to follow suit. Everyone seems to be heading to the double doors along the far wall, which I remember from years of ditching gym as leading to the hall just outside the library, where the school hadn't had enough in the budget at the time to place a security camera. There are several people already in the gym, guys and girls, all fairly young, high schoolers maybe, or at least no older than me. Some hang back, eyeing Renni and me suspiciously, while others run up to the dirt bikers and embrace them, or start a conversation. Me and Renni make like to follow the Nick Fury guy out of the double doors, but he turns on his heel and bends down a little to glower at us.

"Uh uh, ladies," he sneers. "Dinner is a formal affair. Or at least, not a farmhouse pig trough." He points his considerable nose at the ceiling and sniffs at us. "No, you won't do. The locker rooms are over there. Get yourselves cleaned up."

I really can't be too angry at this guy for pointing out the obvious: Renni and me do stink, and we're not looking too pretty either, having just spent the better part of at least a half an hour rolling around in the mud and the rain, and, later, some zombie matter. But when I look to Renni to shrug it off and smirk his comment away, she is fuming.

"Who the fuck do you think you are, man?" She pokes him in his barrel chest with her finger, leaving an indentation in his wet shirt. "We don't take shit from you."

Nick fury is unfazed. "You do if you want to eat a decent meal. But, of course, you're welcome to leave anytime." He flips up the flap on his breast pocket and retrieves a slightly less soggy stogie. He sticks it between his teeth and bites off the end. The kid with the bucket is magically beside him again, all too eager to catch the clipped end.

"We don't need you," Renni starts to say, but I elbow her ribs and give her a look. *We need to get to the tunnels,* my look says. *Maybe this guy can help us out.* Too bad Renni has kind of a hard time reading minds. "What, Devin?"

"We are kind of smelly," I say, beseeching. Renni huffs, but turns away from the guy, relinquishing her hold on the debate. I look at the guy, who has just finished lighting the end of his cigar with a lighter shaped like a miniature .44 Magnum. "We'll meet you in the cafeteria in ten minutes, okay?"

He puffs on the cigar, blowing out smoke like a fog machine. "Make it twenty. Don't rush yourselves."

"What's your name, anyway? I keep calling you Nick Fury in my head."

His laugh thunders out of the very core of him. He pokes himself in the eye patch with his thumb. "Is it the eye patch?"

"No," Renni chimes in, deadpan. "It's your striking resemblance to Samuel L. Jackson."

The guy laughs again, and shakes his smoking cigar in Renni's direction. "You resemble somebody as well." He sticks the cigar back into his smiling mouth. "Fury's fine with me. See you in twenty, ladies."

He aboutfaces out the door, and Renni and me trod over to the locker room doors. "I hate that guy," Renni hisses.

"He could be a white Samuel L. Jackson," I say. "Pre-*Jurassic Park.*"

In the locker room, I go straight for my old locker, out of habit, I guess. It's in the corner closest to the showers. I see a ghostly image of myself as a freshman, looking down at the floor as I unbuttoned my shirt to change into my gym clothes, pausing to steal brief surreptitious glances at the half-naked, towel-wrapped girls coming and going from the shower room. The locker now has someone else's combination lock on it, and I kick it for no reason.

"Okay, so we're supposed to shower," Renni says to the wall, tracing someone's indecipherable graffiti with her finger. "And then change into what clothes, exactly?"

As if on cue, a tiny old woman scuttles into the locker room like a turtle bearing gifts. She places two sets of folded black clothes on the bench in front of us and then backs away shyly, never making eye contact.

After a beat, Renni says, "That was weird."

I pick through the clothes, holding up a black cotton sleeve. "Uniforms are kind of drab."

Then the air becomes weighty with the sudden burden of awkwardness. There's no more stalling to be done; we have our change of clothes and we have our fresh towels, hanging near the shower room entrance. We're expected to shower, but are we expected to shower together? And if we shower together, are we expected to not look at each other? Or can we look at each other, but no touching? Or can we touch each other, but no looking? Is twenty minutes enough time for a quickie? I mean, sure, okay, we got caught up in the heat of some ridiculous, hurtful argument that maybe cut deeper than either of us meant for it to, and we expressed our hurt (and our desperation not to be hurt) through the copious use of tongues and hands in certain places. But that was then (like, maybe fifteen minutes ago) and this is now, and now we're looking at each other like, who undresses first?

"Should we just go in with our clothes on?" Renni asks, smirking a little.

I shake my head and laugh, acknowledging how ridiculous it is to feel this awkward, but still feeling awkward nevertheless. "I know, right."

"Look, I'll go first," Renni says, pulling her mucked up t-shirt off over her head in one fluid movement, and dropping it onto the floor. "You can wait, and go after me, if you want."

She unbuttons her camo pants without looking at me, concentrating instead on removing the contents of her pockets and grouping everything together with her axe and rifle under the bench. She grabs a towel hanging from the rack and turns into the shower room, waiting until she's out of sight to slip off her bra and panties. She kicks them out onto the floor, and seconds later, I hear the rush of water as she turns on the shower.

Well. Here I am.

Gah. Fuck. Why does everything have to be so hard? I sit down on the bench to contemplate this, to tally it up. As of now I have two (2) relatively large chunks of flesh missing from various body parts as a result of a couple of hungry zombies, one (1) cheating girlfriend whom I claim to have forgiven (but then what the hell was all that back in the field with Renni?), probably a little less than four (4) hours to get out of this forsaken town before the government napalms it, and exactly one (1) woman who gives a damn about me enough to stick by me and make out with me even after I've both broken her nose and puked in her mouth. What the hell am I still doing sitting out here?

My clothes are off in a matter of seconds. I leave my bandages on because the wounds are kind of gross to look at and that would defeat the purpose of my bold charging into the shower room. Of course, once I get into the room, my plan to sweep up sexily behind Renni and take her like some beefed up minotaur out of a paranormal romance novel completely shrivels up like the skin on my toes that is already beginning to prune in the mixture of heat and moisture. I try not to stare at Renni's naked body as I go to the shower on her left and turn on the hot water, adjusting the cold with a concentration that rivals Michelangelo's, struggling beneath the Sistine Chapel.

Finally, I get it just right, and then I just stand there.

"There's no shampoo," Renni says. I look at her, looking at me, making no attempt to hide just exactly what she's looking at.

"You're gorgeous," I say before I can stop myself.

Renni smiles. "Are you sure you're really looking at me?"

I stare harder, stare right into her eyes. "I'm sure."

"Then come here," she says, and takes a small step back, inviting me into her stream.

I turn the water in my shower off and walk slowly over to her. The hot water from her shower only cascades over one side of me, my bad side, the bandages over my wounds soaking through, the warmth flooding that side of my body with relief, but leaving my entire right side trembling in the relative cold, sprouting gooseflesh. Renni's skin seems unaffected by either the warmth or the cold. She stands less than a foot away from me, her shallow breathing indicated by the rise and fall of her immaculately toned stomach, which for some reason I can't look away from. I want to look at her face but I am too nervous. I have all these questions spinning through my head that I really don't want any answers to: what are we doing? what does she want? what do I want? what about Carmelle? I'm pretty much a top, Renni probably is too, how is this going to work?

Renni reaches out and scrapes her nails lightly across the skin of my scalp, through my wet hair, but that's the only touch she allows me. "You're too young for me," she says.

"I don't see how that's relevant."

She laughs, and looks down at her feet, for the first time behaving like she might also be nervous. "This doesn't have to be anything, you know?" she says, still not looking at me. She hugs her arms to herself and shrugs, looking at the wall, speaking into the steaming water. "It can just be a dream."

It's easier to make an advance when she isn't looking at me. I take one step closer to her, which presses our stomachs ever so slightly together. Her arms still crossed over her chest, I press my own breasts into her forearms. Keeping my arms at my sides, I lean in, nuzzling my chin in her shoulder, essentially hugging her with only my neck. She rubs her cheek against my ear, and smells my hair. I can't see her face, but I imagine her eyes are closed, as mine are.

"I just feel," she says, her whisper dissipating in the steam so that I have to strain to catch her words, "I just feel…undone."

There are no words to speak after this. She's nailed exactly how I've felt since the first night Carmelle held her headache before her like a shield between us in our bed. And now the only thing left to do is to nail each other.

Except, we don't get that far. She unlaces her arms from her chest and pulls me into her, and we embrace, moving our mouths to each other and kissing first softly, tentatively, then more intensely. Our hands rove, our lips smack and press and pull, our tongues taste throats, lips, skin, tears, steam. But neither of us makes the move to take it further; her hands stay firmly above my waist, and I copy her.

Whatever happened in that field earlier was different than this; that was retaliation—against the people who hurt us, who weren't there to bear the brunt, so we had no choice but to turn to the closest warm body. This—here, now, wrapped up deep within each other—this is consolation.

I don't know how long we would have stayed like that, but it feels like we could do this forever, if it weren't for the water abruptly shutting off. The lights go out half a second later. We pull our heads back from each other, but keep our bodies close.

"What the hell?" Renni says.

It's pitch dark with no windows in the locker rooms. I can't even see the outline of anything. I tilt my head to listen but only hear the faint sound of leftover water dripping from the shower head. I feel Renni's heart picking up speed against my own.

"Power outage," I breathe. "We should find the others."

We find each other's hands in the darkness and slowly make our way out of the shower room, following the walls back to the lockers. We grope around until we feel the pile of folded clothes. It's quite a circus act, trying to dress in the dark, feeling for shirt tags to make sure they're on right side out, measuring waistlines of pants to make sure we've grabbed the right ones before putting them on, following the curve of a shoe with our fingers so we don't don two lefts or two rights. Renni scoops up a few of her weapons, and I grab my knife and handgun from my old jeans. Finally, we make it out into the gymnasium.

The lights are out here, too, and no one is milling about, as far as we can see. There's a little bit of light shining in through the small square windows in the doors leading out into the hall. We follow this beacon and exit out into the hall. Our hair is still wet and sticking to our faces or all tangled and fraying out, we look ridiculous. Despite my best efforts, I've put on my shirt backwards. I pull my arms into the shirt to turn it around, and that's when a young, skinny blonde dressed in the requisite black uniform comes around the corner.

She lowers her rifle when she sees us. "The boss sent me to find you. You okay?"

We only nod in response. "What's going on?" Renni asks.

"Power outage," the woman says, confirming my theory. "Don't worry, we've set up a back-up generator, but it's not powerful enough to extend through the whole school. Come on, the boss is waiting for you in the cafeteria."

We follow her around a few bends in the halls to the cafeteria, even though I could easily lead the way with my eyes closed. My locker was on the second floor, near the computer labs, surrounded by all the other quiet outcasts and A/V geeks. The popular kids, the ones who played sports or instruments or went to parties, all seemed to have lockers on the first floor, nearest the cafeteria. I would walk by them only twice a day, at lunch time, and be completely ignored. I couldn't decide, at the time, if this was better or worse than being picked on.

Now the halls are empty, the lockers standing alone and innocent near the cafeteria entrance, no one to turn their combination locks, no one to lean casually against them while they test out the flirtation techniques they picked up in the latest issue of *Cosmo* over the weekend. We pass them swiftly, and enter through the inward-swinging double doors of the cafeteria.

Most of the rectangular plastic tables have been upended against the row of windows that faces out into the quad. As I suspected when we drove into the parking lot earlier, the windows have been blacked out, though it looks like they were just directly painted over with a few thick coats of black paint. The doors that lead out into the quad are similarly blockaded, and there's a stocky woman stationed there as a guard, peering out into the darkened concrete yard through a hole in the paint only big enough to fit one squinting eye.

The other tables have been set up in a hard-edged circle in the center of the cafeteria, surrounding the lone circular table at which now sits our very own Nick Fury. There are a few people eating at the other tables, keeping their conversations low and private, not even looking up as we enter the room. Nick Fury eats alone. He spots us coming in through the doors and waves us over.

"What will you have, ladies?" he asks, sweeping a hand over his own tray, which is piled high with microwaved pizza and pudding cups. "We have an absolutely stunning array of frozen pizzas and a fair bit of lasagna. A few vats of Tater Tots. I'm leery of the pre-packaged cheeseburgers, however. They're a mite over their expiration date."

A man draped in a white apron comes out of the kitchen, carrying two trays piled high with what looks like a sample platter of all the foods the school's industrial freezers have to offer. He passes between the outer circle of tables and places the trays gently on the table in front of Renni and me, nods once at each of us, then heads back the way he came, disappearing into the kitchen.

"Ah, well," Fury says, patting the edge of one of the trays. "Why decide when you can have it all?"

The smell of the reheated food suddenly has me salivating, and I dig in. The taste of the various spaghetti sauces erases the trace flavors of Renni's mouth, which is regrettable, but I keep on eating. Renni doesn't touch her food. She lays her weapons on the chair next to her and starts in with her questions.

"Who are you?" she begins the interrogation.

Fury wipes his mouth politely with a small square of paper napkin, making sure to dab especially at the wiry hairs of his beard closest to his lips. "I'm just a man," he says, "trying to protect his family."

Renni looks around at the people eating at the other tables, the others standing, checking the doors, marching along the perimeter with their guns. "These people are your family?"

"You're looking for an origin story? All right." He pushes his tray of half-eaten food to the side and retrieves a half-smoked cigar from his chest pocket. "I was produced inside a lab. My mother, for all intents and purposes, was a turkey baster; my father, a Petri dish; my nanny, an incubator. My genes were culled together from a vast array of history's most perfect warriors; I believe you can trace my heritage back to ancient Samurai warlords, to medieval Romans and the shirtless Greeks, back to even Christ himself. I am the result of centuries of genetic tinkering, of splicing and reordering, of failures and near-misses, to produce the perfect, the most diligent, the most focused, the most single-minded, intuitive, relentless, fearless killer of zombies."

I swallow a chunk of soggy pizza. "What?"

"Me and mine were all created in labs by government scientists to protect the populace in the event of zombie-centric catastrophe, such as the one we find ourselves entrenched in now." He opens his arms to indicate the people all around us in the cafeteria. "These are my genetic brothers and sisters, each created, to varying degrees of success, for the same purpose. We've been living, breathing, eating, shitting zombies since before you were conceived, since Christ was a corporal, since—"

"Wait," I interrupt him. "Since Christ was a corporal?"

He waves his fingers at me, brushing it off. "It's a figure of speech."

"It doesn't make any sense."

"It simply means a long time ago."

"Do you mean 'corporeal'?" Renni asks. "Since Christ was corporeal?"

"Oh," I exclaim, slapping Renni's shoulder. "That makes so much more sense."

"Right?" She says. "Like he's able to be touched—"

"Because he was human at one point," I finish her reasoning for her, "instead of now being like a spirit or whatever."

"Right," she nods.

I look back at Fury. "I think you meant corporeal, definitely."

"Definitely," Renni echoes.

Fury slams a balled fist onto the top of the table, knocking food off all our trays. "That isn't even the point!"

"I'm sorry," I say, picking lasagna noodles off my shirtsleeves. "Keep going with what you were saying."

"You and your siblings were created in a lab," Renni repeats, trying to get him back on track. "By who?"

"Who do you presume?" he asks snidely. He produces his revolver-shaped lighter, and almost immediately the kitchen doors swing open, releasing the ten-year-old boy with his blue bucket extended excitedly in front of him. He runs up to our table, all smiles, and patiently waits by Fury's side as he sucks on the freshly lit cigar. Its smoke smells like bad breath and Cheetos, but I just try to breathe through my mouth.

"Our very own American government," Fury goes on. "Why create an entire race of zombie hunters when there are no zombies to hunt? The zombie virus, which only infects dead tissue, was initially conceived as a biological weapon during World War the Second. But, due to some bureaucratic bullshit, was never fully launched. Sure, they field-tested it on a few corpses, but that's as far as the project ever got. Until now.

"Me and mine were created as a fail-safe, in case the virus ever backfired or got out of control, or fell into enemy hands. All in all, we are only a small army, about two hundred and fifty of us. A mere fraction of that followed me in my defection, thirty-two soldiers and this little fellow here." He pauses to once again tousle the kid's shaggy hair.

"Defected?" Renni prompts.

"When the alarm first sounded in the subterranean levels of Fort Wagner Air Force Base two hundred miles from here, where our numbers reside, I knew something was amiss. The attacks hadn't even started yet and we were being called up, instructed where to go and what to do. They pointed us to this town on a containment mission, procedures for which we had been rigorously drilled on for the past few weeks. I found this curious. An advance team of us arrived two days ago, and waited. I had a lot of time to think and form theories during that holding period, and the theory I struck on, the theory that stuck, was that the government got bored, waiting around for another Great War to unleash their newfangled weapons. They got tired of controlled field tests, experiments involving no risks and zero variables. So they released the virus on the unsuspecting public, on this town, on you. And sent us in to clean it up."

My appetite has completely left me at this point, and the smell of all the greasy food in front of me makes me sick. Renni squeezes my knee comfortingly underneath the table.

"So the government did this?" Renni asks, her voice a rasp of rising anger.

"That's my theory," Fury says, sucking on his cigar. "And I don't like it. Our people shouldn't be the guinea pigs in this, innocent Americans confronted with this much trauma. It's not right. I don't want any part in this little experiment, but I also want to take down zombies. Old habits die hard, as they say. I did get that saying right, didn't I?"

"The Army is set to invade this city at six a.m," Renni says. She looks at the numerical clock mounted on the wall above the cafeteria entrance doors. "That's in three hours."

Fury nods. "Right. Since we defected, effectively abandoning the project, the brass have had a lot of problems on their hands, trying to contain this incident. The second wave of zombie hunters has probably already arrived, but they're still planning. I have no doubt they'll march in here, prepared to take out anything that moves, be it zombie or human. They won't risk infection."

"So that's real?" I ask him, trying not to sound too scared. "If you get bitten or something, you become a zombie?"

Fury looks at me gravely. "Afraid so. The virus mutates from its original state, which attacks the dead tissue, essentially bringing it back to life. Once it passes from one system to another, it becomes a contagion, spreading through living tissue and deteriorating it, killing the afflicted host. Once the host dies, the virus re-launches its attack on the dead tissue, and brings it back to life, so to speak. It's cyclical."

I make an involuntary whimpering sound in the back of my throat. Renni says, "How long does that process take?"

Fury looks back and forth between us, his eyes narrowing. "Has one of you ladies been bitten?"

Thankfully, we are saved from having to answer by a commotion at the cafeteria doors. A group of five black-attired militia guys—elite zombie-hunting soldiers, we now know—comes marching in, forming a very military style V-shaped formation. Everyone at the other tables stop their conversations and stand up. The V marches through the outer perimeter of tables and approaches our circular table. The little boy with the bucket sinks back a little, his smile erased. Nick Fury does not stand up.

He looks at the militia guys with some mild disdain. "Report," he commands.

"Sir." The tip of the V steps forward and salutes. "We've collected a specimen, sir."

Fury's eyebrows perk up. He takes the cigar slowly out of the corner of his mouth. "Fully intact?"

The militia guy nods. "Fully intact, sir."

The excited gleam in Fury's eyes cannot be contained. He tosses the stub of his cigar carelessly behind him; the little boy has to dive painfully onto his stomach to catch it in his outstretched bucket. Fury stands up. "Is the lab set up?"

"Being prepped now."

"Let's go," Fury pushes away from the table. Renni shoots up from her seat and grabs his arm at the crook of his elbow. He eyes her, and the four militia men aim their rifles at her.

I stand up slowly, cautiously, sending worried glances at the gunmen, then at Fury, then at Renni, finally back to the gunmen.

"You have some sort of objection?" Fury asks, his voice sounding bemused, but his face looking stern, angry.

"What's going on?" she demands, seemingly unfazed by the danger she's put herself in by not letting go of the commander's arm. "What's he talking about, a specimen?"

Fury smiles then, inviting yet sharp. All at once, he reminds me of a bear, the way Biff Tipping reminded me of a bear; big and scary on the outside, soft and warm on the inside, but unpredictable. "But of course," he says through his large teeth stained brown from tobacco. "You ladies are invited along to observe."

Renni doesn't seem to want to let go of his arm. I reach out and touch her arm. "Come on, Renni," I say, softly. "He'll explain on the way." I look at him. "Won't you?"

Fury salutes me with three fingers, like a Boy Scout. "On my honor," he says. Renni reluctantly releases his arm.

The gunmen lower their rifles. "This way, Mister Machina."

We follow them out of the cafeteria. As we're mounting the steps to the second floor, I ask Fury, "Mister Machina?"

He smiles tightly. "Ah, you've discovered my true name. Deus Ex Machina. It's Greek. But I like your name for me better. I prefer it."

We walk through the dimly lit halls of the second floor until we come to the closed doors of the chemistry lab. Two women stand guard like sentries on either side of the door. Fury instructs his men to remain in the hall and ushers us inside in front of him.

In the room, we are immediately confronted with a bit of that trauma Fury was lamenting our exposure to just moments ago. A zombie lies prone atop a lab table, his clothes tattered and torn, his exposed limbs, which have not quite attained the greenish hue of prolonged death, strapped to the table by yards and yards of duct tape. In fact, his whole body is crisscrossed with it, even his neck, so that he can only lift his head a few inches from the table. When we enter, he looks at us with those deadened, glass-like eyes, opens his mouth, black with other people's blood, and greets us with a low, rattling moan.

"Jesus," Renni breathes, grabbing hold of my arm. We both stop in our tracks and just stare at the zombie. The smell is atrocious, the view even worse. From the corner of the lab, a man in a white lab coat, lower face covered by a white paper mask, approaches the table, brandishing a bone saw.

"Mister Machina," he greets our commander, who has come in behind us and circles to the head of the zombie lying on the table. He appears neither shocked or concerned to see this zombie lying here, but rather quite eager.

"Doctor," Fury says, returning the greeting.

"Shall we begin?" the doctor asks, tapping the dull handle of the bone saw against the fingers of his latex-gloved hand.

"By all means," Fury says.

"Stop!" Renni shouts. The zombie's moan grows to match the volume of her voice. "You promised us an explanation."

Fury sighs, and turns to us. "Of course, ladies. My apologies. I forgot myself in light of this exciting development."

"Exciting?" I shiver, and move closer to Renni.

"I realize it must seem fairly macabre to you both," Fury says, stepping in front of the table so that the upper half of the zombie is blocked from view, but we can still hear his long, continuous moan. "But believe me, our experiments here will benefit not only you both, but all of the survivors."

"There are other survivors?" Renni asks.

"Of course," Fury says. "That's why we defected in the first place, to help the survivors, get them out of the city before the government comes in to collect their own specimens, infected civilians, like you." He looks at me when he says it. My fear catches in my throat. "We've collected a small group of survivors, awaiting instructions in the library downstairs. We plan to help them escape at the very last moment, when the government's soldiers, our comrades, launch their first sweep, the maneuvers of which we are all aware from our training drills. We'll get them all out, no doubt, but some have been infected and we don't know what to do for them. Not yet."

He steps back to reveal the zombie, extending an open palm to him, like he's a prize on display for some game show. "This unfortunate individual will help us discover a cure for the infection. I'm certain the government has one, but they won't use it, not for this mere trial run. All your lives are expendable to them. But not to me. You're Americans. My sisters in nationality. I refuse to lose a single one of you. Of course, we were all bred to be soldiers, killers, not exactly scientists. But we'll do our best. Now that we have a fully intact specimen, things should run much more smoothly. Do you understand?"

"Not entirely," Renni admits.

"Ah," Fury says with a renewed smile, "then you are not a scientist, either."

As if this should satisfy us, Fury turns back to the doctor and the prone zombie. "Make the first incision."

My wounds begin to throb again and the ache travels through my body and into my head. I close my eyes as the doctor nods and lowers the bone saw against the zombie's forehead. Renni wraps me in her arms and for a second, I get lost in her, the closeness and the solidity of her body, the familiar musk of her skin. Then the screaming starts.

The guards stationed outside burst into the room behind us. My eyelids fly open as my heart stops. Fury is against the wall, .44. Magnum—not the little replica lighter but an actual beast of a handgun—drawn and aimed, slightly unsteadily, at the zombie on the table. The zombie who is currently screaming as a stream of bright red blood runs in rivulets down the side of his head.

"Motherfucker!" the zombie screams. "That fucking *hurts*!"

Chapter 8

A Zombie for Your Thoughts

ZOMBIE LORE, MUCH LIKE THE VIRUS FURY TOLD US OUR government has created for use as a biological weapon, mutates every few years to suit the needs of those who invoke it. As I've covered earlier, zombies were once summoned forth by witches and their ilk, to act as tools with virtually no autonomy of their own, maiming and killing according to their master's whims, not their own. Spells gave way to viruses, air- or blood-borne pathogens that reawakened dead tissue, reanimating corpses and turning humans into soulless monsters. Some lore even insists that you can take the whole "undead" thing out of the zombie equation, like they essentially did in that movie *28 Days Later*, but there is much debate about this.

However, one thing there has never been a debate over—never, ever, not once, not even a little—is the ability of a zombie to speak: they simply cannot do it.

Yet, here we are.

The zombie on the table stops screaming, giving way instead to a kind of dry sobbing. He struggles against his restraints, but the duct tape holds fast. He blinks some of the blood out of his eyes, then suddenly jerks his head to the left, to look at the doctor who still brandishes the bone saw. Then he jerks his head to the right and looks at me and Renni. His eyes no longer look glassy and lifeless, but they do look bloodshot and crazed.

"What the hell is going on here?" he booms. "Answer me!" He scans the room again, wriggling his head around as wildly as the restraints will allow him. "Somebody answer me, goddammit!"

"Well," Fury says, pushing away from the wall and lowering his gun. "This certainly is interesting."

"Who are you people?" the zombie continues to shout. "What are you doing to me? Where am I? Help! Help!"

Gracefully, Fury takes one solid step forward and cracks the zombie in the side of his face with the butt of his Magnum. The zombie's head whips back with the impact, and then lolls to a stop, his mouth silenced.

"Did you kill him?" Renni screams, furious.

"He's already dead," Fury reasons back.

"Bullshit!" Renni lets go of me and runs up to the zombie's table. Fury waves back the militia men, who have trained their rifles once again on Renni. They fall back under Fury's silent command.

Renni rips open the zombie's already shredded shirt and presses her ear to his chest, simultaneously ripping at the duct tape that binds his neck to the table. She manages to get it loose enough to dig two fingers under the tape. After a couple of seconds, she whips back up.

"He's got a fucking pulse!"

Dubiously, Fury goes to the zombie's side to check for himself. His face reveals nothing as he runs his own fingers under the tape. He motions for the doctor to check, and he too places his hands on the zombie's flesh.

"Yep," the doctor confirms. "His heart's beating."

"Impossible," Fury exclaims. He runs his hands over the rest of the zombie's body, tearing at his pants leg until he reveals the wound on his calf. "There," Fury says, pointing at the bloody teeth marks with the barrel of his Magnum. "You see? He was bitten. He's a zombie."

"Just a sec," the doctor says, pulling down his paper mask to reveal a frowning mouth. He leans over the body and uses the dull handle of the bone saw to scrape at the dried blood caked over the bite wound. The leg twitches under this new stimulant. It doesn't take long for fresh blood to seep out of the uncovered wound, bright red, like a warning.

"For fuck's sake," Nick Fury says, backing off and scratching his eye patch in consternation.

"I don't understand," Renni says. "I thought bites transmitted the virus."

"Yes, yes," Fury nods his head vigorously. "Undoubtedly, they do. At least, the virus we've all been trained to fight against does. Most certainly."

"So you're saying this isn't the same virus?" I ask. All eyes turn to look at me. "This is something new?"

Fury thinks for a minute, chewing the insides of his cheeks. The doctor puts down the bone saw, snaps off his gloves. One of the militia guys coughs into his elbow. "Or," Fury says, turning back to the never-really-was-a zombie. "It's not a virus at all."

"Then what the fuck is it?" The forcefulness of my voice surprises even me, but Fury responds well to it.

He snaps his fingers at the doctor. "Get the smelling salts."

The doctor rummages noisily through some drawers as I become increasingly impatient. I feel my body seizing up, preparing to betray me. Everything starts to feel heavy, to feel like a chore, breathing, blinking, swallowing. A cold sweat breaks out all over me. Finally, the doctor finds the salts and brings them over to Fury. Fury waves it in front of the nose of the man on the table. The man awakens with a jolt that morphs into a sneeze.

"Where am I?" he asks, kind of groggily.

Thankfully, Fury's patience has grown as thin as my own. He plants his hands roughly on either side of the man's head and looms over him, so that all the man can see is his large, hairy, one-eyed, imposing face. "Who are you?" Fury demands, voice booming, punching the table for emphasis. "What's the last thing you remember? Something bit you. What bit you? Tell me!"

The man coughs a little and struggles against his restraints again, but only briefly, until he finally realizes there's nowhere for him to go. He starts to cry, to whimper, but he manages, through stops and starts, to tell his story:

"It's all a fog, man, I don't know. I was…I was visiting my grandmother's grave. She just died a few months ago and I go once a month to check on it, to make sure…make sure the grounds crew is keeping it maintained, you know? They neglect the graves no one visits, I know this, I've seen it, every time I visit, I see it. I loved my grandma, oh man, I loved her. She was great, she…. I owe her, man, you know. So I go to check on the grave, and this time…this time…it was disturbed. I remember walking up to it and knowing something was wrong, something…. As I got closer I saw what it was…the earth had been dug up, and then replanted. It was rough…it looked terrible. I was upset. I was going to go tell someone, someone who worked for the cemetery, you know, to come out here and fix it, but then…. Then…."

The man sputters through his sobs and cuts off. But then Fury slams his fists next to his head again, and the man starts up, as if by hitting the table Fury had punched his "on" switch.

"I saw my grandmother. Oh man, grandma. 'Grandma,' I said, even though I didn't really believe it was her, but…but…she was wearing her purple dress, the one with the veil, the one we…we…the one we buried her in. Oh man. She was coming toward me, kind of unsteady like, reaching out to me. I couldn't see her face under the veil but I could…I could smell her. I knew something was wrong, something was terribly, terribly wrong, but there she was, reaching out to me. She fell down, and I ran to her, it was instinct, you know, to help my grandma up. I got close and she reached out. Oh man, the shivers that ran through me when she latched onto my ankle with her bone-dead fingers, oh fuck, oh man, like a ghost walking over my own grave, oh man. I tried to run then but she was strong. She pulled my foot to her and she bit me. Right through my Dockers, man, I love these pants! I yanked free but by then…by then…there were more people…people like her…dead people, in their funeral clothes, all over the hills of the cemetery, coming after me. I knew then, I knew, as I was running full tilt the hell away from them, I knew what they were. Zombies."

The man sputters and stops again. Instead of slamming the table again, Fury leans in mere centimeters from the guy's mouth and prompts, gruffly but less violently, "And that's the last thing you remember?"

The man shakes his head slowly. "No. No. I remember sitting in my car. I couldn't get my fingers to work. I was trying to put the keys into the ignition but I couldn't hold onto them. Kept dropping 'em. My leg hurt something awful, kept cramping up. And then...then I felt this rumbling, deep down inside me. This hunger. I remember looking out the window at all them dead people, moving around on broken feet, and thinking, 'This is it. I'm one of you now.' And that's the last thing before everything went black."

One of the militia guys behind us clears his throat and speaks up. "Sir? We did find him a few blocks away, near Pine Fork Cemetery. He was lying next to a stalled Lexus, eating the guts of a dead dog."

"Oh God," the man exclaims, struggling once more. "Oh man, fuck, I ate a dog? Oh God, what else did I do?" He licks his tongue out around his bottom lip, tasting the old blood on his chin for the first time. "Oh man, no, oh God. I'm a vegetarian! I'm gonna be sick." His stomach makes a loud gurgling sound and convulses against the duct tape. Fury moves lightning quick away from his face, and just in time too, as he begins to projectile vomit. Except the vomit is shot straight up because of how the man's head is secured, so it has nowhere to go except straight back down. The man sobs and vomits again as the stuff splatters back onto his own face. It's a cycle I don't see ending any time soon, and don't particularly think I need to be here for. I bolt.

No one tries to stop me. I take some random corners until I find an open, quiet room that smells like old book pages and lemon-scented floor cleaner. This room has a little supply closet behind a row of desks and I go in and shut the door. The light is out in here and I just sit with my back against the wall, sandwiched between a box of computer paper and a tub of papier-mâché paste.

What the fuck is going on? The once-zombie, or never-really-was-a zombie's words echo through my brain, which has heated up with pain, exhaustion, and more than a little confusion. I try to review the facts but there don't seem to be any. No one knows what's going on, and we have less than three hours to figure something out or we're all dead.

There's a small knock on the door. "It's me," Renni says through it. I lean forward and twist the knob, pushing the door open a little. There's a little moonlight to see her by, coming through the classroom windows. "You want to be alone?"

"I can be alone with you," I say.

She comes into the closet and sits down cross-legged in front of me, closing the door behind her. There's barely enough room for both of us; our legs are practically on top of each other. In the dark, her hands find mine and hold on tight.

"This shit just gets crazier and crazier," she says, sighing.

"Yeah," I say. I can't think of anything else to say so we just sit there in silence, listening to each other breathe.

Finally, Renni says, "Psychosomatic."

"What?"

"That guy in there," she explains. "The pseudo-zombie. It was a psychosomatic reaction to a traumatic experience. It was all in his head. He was overwhelmed. Can't beat 'em? Join 'em."

"Is that your clinical assessment?" I ask, not trying to sound like a dick, but come on. Psychosomatic? That's not her word.

"You're constantly underestimating me, chica," Renni says. I can't see her face in the dark so I can't tell if she's pissed, and her voice reveals nothing. "You listened to the same story I did. What did you think of it?"

"No, your theory sounds right," I say, my voice betraying everything. "It's just...it's scarier."

Renni lets go of one of my hands to massage my knee with her thumb. "Why is it scarier?"

I'm starting to cry, not even making any effort to hide it. I haven't been able to hide anything from this woman since the moment I met her, why try to start now?

"Because," I say wetly, "because if there's one of him, then there's probably more of him. More people who think they're zombies. More people going around out there, hurting even more people, and those people thinking *they're* zombies, and everyone just fucking everybody else up. And then there's us, people like us and literally us, out there shooting them because *we* think they're zombies, we think they're already dead, so we're killing them, just shooting them like it's a fucking video game, murdering—"

"Hey, hey." Renni stops my rant before it can get any more hysterical. I'm breathing hard and my face is a mess, and I'm glad she can't see me. She holds my face in her hands and wipes at my cheeks with the backs of her knuckles, but the tears keep coming. "I get why that might scare you, but, Devin, listen. Try to remember, okay? Remember what those zombies looked like—"

"—but they weren't zombies!"

"Shh, shh, listen. Remember what they looked like, outside of the porn shop, and the guy in the furniture store. You remember?"

I do remember. "Dirty," I sob. "Smelly, old." My hysteria has reduced my communication skills to that of a monosyllabic first grader.

"That's right." Renni smoothes my hair back behind my ears. "And what else?"

I scrunch my eyes shut, thinking back. "Dusty. Broken. Dripping. Rotting."

"Like they'd been buried," Renni says.

I open my eyes. "Like they'd been buried," I repeat.

"Because they were buried," Renni says. "A long time ago. Those ones we fought, those ones we put down? None of them looked like that man over there in that lab, did they? No. Because the ones we put down, Devin, honey, those were zombies. The real fucking zombies who started all this shit. You got that?"

My breathing gradually calms down as Renni continues to stroke my face. I start hiccuping, and this makes me laugh. I sniff back my tears. "You called me honey," I say.

Suddenly her face is directly in front of mine. She whispers, "You got a problem with that?"

My spine begins to tingle. I shake my head before I remember she can't see me in the dark. "Not at all." I start to call her "pumpkin," but she kisses me, cutting off the term of endearment in the middle.

The kiss doesn't last long, but it's sweet. She pulls her lips back first, but keeps her forehead resting against mine. I can smell her breath as she speaks, which smells like how she tastes, which is like Tater Tots.

"We still have to get the hell out of here," she says.

"But that Mister Machina guy was wrong," I say. "Whatever caused these zombies, it wasn't the government's virus."

"Unless they created a new strain they didn't tell him about."

"I guess that's possible."

"But that's not your theory?"

I shake my head, moving hers along with mine. "I don't think so. Why would they hide what they were doing from the very soldiers they've been training for the sole purpose of being able to defend against what they're doing? If this was an experiment, it was to test out these soldier's ability to contain the virus should it ever be used against us, not to test out the virus's ability to trick even their own soldiers. It wouldn't benefit them at all, to create something so amorphous that it can't be brought down by their own guys."

"Then what's your theory?"

That's when it hits me, that's when I know. The thing I've been thinking all along, alluding back to in my own internalized history of zombification. "Someone summoned them."

To my surprise, Renni doesn't laugh in my face. "Didn't I tell you it was some whack job just trying some shit out in his basement? Didn't I say that from the beginning?"

"Maybe. I don't remember."

"I did. I said it was some bored scientist with a god complex."

"You didn't say that exactly."

"Close enough."

"Anyway, summoning them is a little different from creating them in your basement."

"Right, sure. But if they were summoned, there must have been a purpose, besides general chaos and destruction."

"Why do you say that?"

"I don't know," I hear the fabric of her shirt crinkle together as she shrugs. "Is summoning a zombie very easy to do?"

"Probably not."

"Then whoever did it must have had a very good reason to go through all the trouble. Don't you think?"

Just then, the door opens behind Renni and light from the classroom spills into the closet. She peels her face back from mine and twists her body around to see who has disturbed us. It's Mister Nick Fury, AKA Mister Machina, standing with hands on hips, fresh stogie jutting out of the corner of his mouth.

"Okay, ladies," he says. "Play time's over. We're heading out."

Renni stands up, then helps me to my feet. "What do you mean?"

"I'm sorry, I thought you understood English." Fury laughs at his own joke. "Evidently this little zombie problem isn't ours to fix. Our government didn't cause it, so me and mine no longer feel responsible to end it. But we did make a commitment to get any survivors out of here, and we're not going back on that. We don't have to worry about infection anymore, so we can just walk out through the decontamination blockades. Let's go."

"Wait," Renni says. "But they think there's still an infection."

"They won't after we talk to them, and present them with evidence of our man formerly known as zombie." He plucks the cigar out of his mouth and squints at us. "What's the matter? Don't you ladies want to get out of here? Put this whole mess behind you? Get back to your families and loved ones?"

Renni doesn't say anything. I pipe up, "What about the other psychosomatic zombies? All those people hobbling around out there, injured and delirious, thinking they're zombies? We can't just leave them all out there."

"We don't have the manpower to wrangle up all those pseudos," Fury says, stuffing the cigar back in his cheek. "But you don't have to worry about them. Once we explain everything to the Army out there, they'll reverse their tactics, send in a couple of rescue teams to obtain and rehabilitate the afflicted. They'll send in another team to ascertain the identities of the actual zombies, and take them down."

"How can you know that?" I ask.

"Because it's what I would do," he says, puffing up his chest. "And I used to be in charge of this mission. All us military rats tend to think the same when it comes to strategy. Even those of us not raised in a lab. Anyway, you don't really have to come with us, it's safe to stay behind now. But I'm offering you a ride, if you want to take it. Meet us in the gymnasium in twenty if you're coming with us."

He gives us the three-finger Boy Scout salute again, turns on his heel, and marches out of the classroom. The yellow lights stay on in the classroom, and under them, Renni and I look each other over.

"Well," I say, knocking my wrists against the sides of my waist. "I guess it's over."

"Kind of anti-climactic," Renni says.

As if to emphasize that the danger is indeed behind us, a chorus of school children begins to sing. Their earnest altos rise up from the floor below us, vibrating our feet. Renni and me both look down. I can't make out words, only harmony and pitch, but it sounds like they are singing some sort of Christmas carol. I can only assume all this singing is the jubilant reaction of the other survivors Fury and his soldiers rounded up before coming to our rescue. Probably he delivered the good news and this is how they are rejoicing.

"That's fucking annoying," Renni says under her breath, in the tone of voice she might use with a cat who just dropped a freshly decapitated mouse proudly at her feet. We meet each other's eyes and our laughter boils out of us like a pot left on the stove a minute too long.

I swipe at the moisture building in the corners of my eyes. "Shit, Renni," I say. "I'm gonna miss you."

Renni waves this sentiment away. "By the next zombie outbreak, you'll have forgotten all about me."

The singing below us fades away as the survivors are marched from their holding pattern in the library to the gymnasium. Very distantly, we can hear engines starting up.

"Here," Renni says, scanning the room. She trots to the front of the room. "Wait here."

But of course I don't wait. I follow her, leaning my butt against a left-handed school desk in the front row. When I was a student here, I always sat in the front row, unless we had assigned seats. Sure, it made the back of my head a primary target for spit wads and partially chewed gum, but it also allowed me to focus on the teacher and the lesson, to block out the unseemliness all around me, and to see only what I wanted to see. Now, I focus in on Renni, who is busy rifling through the drawers of the teacher's desk. She emerges with a thick, black Sharpie marker.

She comes around the desk to stand in front of me. "Give me your arm." She curls her fingers at me impatiently.

I hold my right arm to my chest protectively, pouting a little. "What for?"

"Come on," Renni says. "Trust me."

How can I not, after all of this? She takes my wrist and turns my arm over, so that the smooth skin of the underside is revealed. She uncaps the marker with her teeth, holding the cap in her cheek like Fury holds his cigars. She begins to write on my arm; the ink of the mark is cold. I shiver.

"What are you writing?"

She slurs around the marker cap in her mouth, "My autograph."

When she's finished I see she's written down ten digits. "Don't let me see that number on some blog, you hear me?" she smirks as she recaps the marker.

I look at my arm as if it's grown scales but I'm not too worried about it; scales are pretty good for guarding your skin against the elements, and reptilian humanoids are kind of cool. Still, it's strange. I pull my gaze away from my arm, finally, and look up at Renni. She's leaning casually back against the teacher's desk, observing me.

"So," I say, clearing my throat, "what will you do? After this."

She raises one eyebrow at me, but looks down, sucking in wet air, drumming her fingers along the ridge of the desktop. "I don't know. Go back to L.A., I guess. This vacation's kind of sucked. Well, most of it. You?"

I look around for some idea of what to say in the posters of George Washington and Mount Rushmore and the map of America adorning the classroom walls. The inanimate objects that fill this room are not very forthcoming tonight. "I think I'll…you know." I shrug, stalling for time. "Just…keep going."

"With Carmelle?" Renni asks, looking at me again.

I soften my own gaze, but confirm, "With Carmelle."

She doesn't say anything then. We lean against our respective desks and listen to the engines downstairs, the motions of tires on linoleum, feet running up and down stairs, marching through hallways. It sounds like the rain is letting up outside. Renni swallows. I swallow. The clock above the door ticks away our remaining minutes together.

"Renni," I start, taking a deep breath. "I wouldn't have survived this without you."

She looks at me for a few seconds, almost long enough for me to cough and try again as if she might have missed what I said, and then she says, "I know. You owe me."

I laugh wetly, kind of more of a snort, and look away, shaking my head, trying to suck the tears back into their rightful, burning place in the center of my chest. "Goddammit, Renni."

I hear her move away from the desk and then my cheek is buried in her hair, partially dry now but still smelling vaguely like the chemically treated water of the school's showers. She wraps her arms tightly around me and hugs me close, careful of my injured shoulder. I return the embrace with everything I have.

"I still don't get it," I say into her earlobe.

"Get what?" Her lips reverberate against my tragus.

"Why you stayed with me. Why you came back."

"Can't we just call it fate?"

"Do you believe in fate?"

She backs her head up just enough for her mouth to tremble against my left temple. "I believe in not ruining a beautiful moment with unanswerable questions."

"But—"

"Shhh," she admonishes, and kisses her way across my forehead—still slightly tender and bruising from my run-in with the dashboard earlier—down my eyes, over my nose, to linger on my lips.

It's our last kiss, and it isn't long or deep enough, but it will have to do. The clock's ticking.

We leave the classroom, hand in hand, and walk through the halls of my old high school like sweethearts, like Homecoming Queens.

As we near the gymnasium, the cacophony of revving engines, jolly singing, and jubilant, shouting voices intensifies. Inside the gym, it's enough to drown out my own conflicting thoughts, for which I am grateful. The wide double doors at the far end of the gym have been flung wide open as if there is nothing left to fear. One by one, a caravan of vehicles buses through them and out into the night: Jeeps carrying the dressed-in-black soldiers, still with their guns raised, and a handful of white golf carts shuttling the unarmed civilian survivors. I recognize a few faces as they queue up to exit: there's Walt, the scrawny eleventh grader who bags my groceries at Whole Foods; there's Edna Mae and Stephen, an elderly couple who caused a big ol' ruckus amongst the church gossipers a while back for moving in together and never marrying (I'm glad to see they made it through this, arms around each other and smiling big, as usual); there's that

family of six who come into Ashbee's at least once a month to stare at the giant HD televisions they'll never be able to afford. I wave to them as they pass, but none of them looks my way.

The dirt bikers circle loudly up to us. Renni tenses a bit, as if preparing for a confrontation, but they stop well short of us. Two riders disembark and take off their helmets. They hold them out to us. "They're yours if you want 'em."

Nick Fury comes up behind us and barks, "Hell yeah, they want 'em!"

Renni drops my hand and takes the sleek black helmet from one of the riders. "You serious?"

"Those two'll ride in the Jeep with me," Fury confirms. He pats his breast pocket for a second, but it appears he is out of cigars. Not to fret though; the boy with the blue bucket appears momentarily, holding a fresh stogie out to his hero.

"What is that all about, anyway?" I ask, figuring this will be the last time I interact with this Fury—or Mister Machina, as it were—so might as well speak my mind.

Fury shrugs and hitches up his belt of bullets, taking the cigar from the kid. "Privileges, my dear." He bites off the end of the cigar, and spits it into the boy's ready bucket—*plunk!* The boy beams. "We all have to carry the blue bucket at some point in our lives. Don't we?"

Before I can respond with more than a half-curious, half-dumb look, Renni calls my name. She's straddling one of the dirt bikes already and proffering the other helmet. "Light a fire under your ass!"

I've never ridden anything with more power than a ten-speed bicycle, but somehow I'm not nervous to try this. The dirt bikes are small, and I figure if I wipe out on one of these tonight, after everything else I've survived, at least the irony will be beautiful.

It's wobbly going at first, but I follow Renni out of the gym without incident, and once in the parking lot she keeps her pace slow so that I can keep up. We're trailing the rest of the convoy a good deal, but I don't really care. I keep my eyes trained on Renni's back, watch the wind rustle her shirt, the chill of the rain still with us, stinging my exposed skin awake. I hug the dirt bike with my legs, trying to drive it by feeling and instinct without overthinking. It's kind of Zen.

Renni decelerates a bit more so that we're riding parallel. We look at each other through the tinted visors of our helmets. I shoot her a thumbs up. She shoots one back. And that's when the zombies attack.

Two of them dart out from the dark, cavernous space between two parked vans, and dive for Renni. They don't time their joint leap quite right, and they end up barreling into the bike's back tire, which sends the whole thing spinning out and throws Renni to the pavement. I desperately try to brake as her bike whips by me, sparks flying as the metal and plastic frame skids across the double yellow line. Finally, my hand finds the brake and I come to an abrupt halt, and jump off, not bothering with the kickstand, or to even turn off the engine. Thirty or so feet back, Renni is on her side, her helmet having flung off when she hit the ground, and the zombies are inches from her, salivating almost as loudly as they're moaning.

I still have my handgun tucked into my pants from after the shower, as well as the hunting knife. My instinct is to go for the gun, but I take up the knife instead. Because these two zombies didn't amble or shuffle or limp to take down Renni, they ran. And zombies simply do not run.

Trusting my impeccable aim to guide me even though I've never thrown a knife like this before, I grip the business end like I've seen in movies and let it rip. Both zombies are crouched low, picking at Renni, who seems to be unconscious. My aim does prove true, but my knife throwing is for shit; the handle *thromps* into the side of one of the zombie's heads, and he stumbles back, knocked off balance. He clutches his head with one hand and moans, until his moan becomes a very audible, "Ow!"

His companion looks up, mouth dripping with Renni's blood and a bit of cloth from her t-shirt, looking quite confused.

"You're not a zombie!" I scream, running up to them. Both dudes look at me. "You're not a fucking zombie, asshole!" I reach the trio and kick the bloody guy in the face. He falls back, clutching his mouth.

"What's going on here?" The other guy whines. He's sitting on his butt now, rocking back and forth, hugging himself. The guy I just kicked starts rolling to and fro, crying.

"Shut up!" I don't have time for either of these guy's issues. I kneel down by Renni and appraise her wounds. It looks like only one pseudo-zombie took a bite out of Renni's forearm, and even that was more cloth than flesh. Her shirt is ripped at the chest where the other pseudo-zombie had tried to scratch his way to something deeper. I roll her onto her back and brush the hair away from her face. She's bleeding from a wound on her forehead, but it's pretty shallow. Her nose is bleeding again, too.

"Renni," I say loudly, shaking her. "Renni."

Some moaning from the side of the road draws my attention. Coming down the block is a band of zombies who look the part; only three or four of them have fully intact faces, at least two of them are shuffling forward on broken ankles, and they're all dressed in their finest drab suits and dresses of muted colors.

"Come on, Renni, you gotta get up!" I slap her cheeks lightly but get no response. I think back to how easy it was to wake her in the hotel room and wish for that ease back. But without it, I have no choice. I punch her in the vagina.

She bolts upright and slugs me across the jaw as she curls up tight to manage the pain. "Fuck," she bellows.

"Zombies!" I shout, pointing with one hand at the rovers who are just now stepping off the curb, and rubbing my jaw with the other.

"Too many of them," Renni quickly assesses. She touches her fingers gingerly to her nose. "Shit, I think I re-broke this."

Then from behind us comes an echo of moans. There's another band, double the size of the first one, pushing in from the opposite side of the street.

"Start shooting!" Renni yells.

I quickly scan this new group. "Not all of them are real zombies!"

Renni leans forward and rips the gun out of my waistband. She positions herself on one knee, leveling the gun over her other leg, holding steady with a two-handed grip, like a pro. She pops off three shots at the first band, skimming a shoulder here, a neck there, but no head shots; the zombies shuffle on.

"Shit, I can't focus!"

"That sounds familiar," I mumble, thinking of her role as my namesake in *Rising Evil*. Her character was bitten and slowly succumbing to the virus, which weakened her ability to focus.

"Oh God," one of the pseudo-zombies, still rolling on the asphalt, starts talking to himself. "Oh God, oh God, oh God." The other pseudo-zombie just starts screaming.

"Renni!" At the sound of my voice, Renni whips around and fires off a shot in the direction of the second band. It goes wild, and the zombie who occasioned my shout, a mite quicker than his friends, reaches us. I kick at his knees and he stumbles to the ground, causing Renni's second shot to whiz over his head and implant itself into the thigh of another zombie. This zombie screams—"My leg!"—and goes down.

"Sorry!" Renni yells at him.

The other zombies realize he isn't one of them and turn on him.

I kick frantically at the pseudo-zombie nearest me. "Get up and fight! You're not a fucking zombie, so get up and fucking fight!"

The zombie I'd kicked before reaches out to grasp my ankle, and I drop my heel into his face, shattering his cheekbone but leaving his brain unharmed. I quickly rectify this by digging my fingers in his disgusting hair and slamming his head into the ground until I hear a slopping splat-sound that makes me gag. He doesn't move, but it's too late anyway; all of a sudden, zombies from both bands are on top of us.

I hear Renni shoot a couple more rounds until the gun runs out of ammo, and then she starts swinging it. We fight with our backs to each other, flailing and screaming, spitting and bleeding, periodically connecting with a pseudo-zombie who wakes up at the hit, and taking a number of scratches and bites ourselves. I'm sure we're going down, but goddammit, we're going down hard.

A noise like thunder breaks through the collective moans of all these zombies, and suddenly we're bathed in bright white light. A second later, I see the bumper of the Jeep just as it connects with my hip. I fly back from the impact, falling onto a couple of sharply dressed older female zombies. I elbow them both simultaneously in their mouths and get back to my feet before the pain of the collision has time to set in my bones.

All around me lie prone zombie bodies and pseudo-zombies. Most of the zombies are quiet, some of them are trying to crawl forward or pull themselves up futilely on their broken legs, and the pseudo-zombies are kind of freaking out. I help Renni up and we stare into the blinding white light.

The lights go off, and in the Jeep I can see now the three most beautiful faces I have ever seen: Cherry in the driver's seat, Brad in the passenger's seat, and Carmelle—sweet, beautiful, complicated Carmelle—standing up in the back, rifle raised high and hair blowing back wildly in the wind.

"I'm sorry," Cherry squeaks out from the driver's seat, turning off the engine. "I don't know how to drive a stick. The brake and the clutch are so close together."

"Cherry," I exclaim. "Get out here and fucking hug me."

"Fuckin' right on, fuck yeah," Brad says. Everyone hops out of the

Jeep and soon I am embraced by six pairs of arms, and one pair of lips, that I hope belong to Carmelle because I've closed my eyes and can't really be sure. Our reunion is cut short by the sound of Renni stomping in zombie brains and kicking pseudo-zombies in the ribs, just to remind them they're alive. When everyone sees her, and she sees them, a silent agreement seems to pass through everyone, and they surge toward her, encasing her in an inescapable three-way bear hug. Despite her initial look of surprise and discomfort, she smiles broadly.

"All right, all right," she pushes them back playfully. "What the hell are we still doing here?"

"She's right," I say. "There could be more coming. Let's head for the state line. Maybe we can catch up with Fury's convoy."

"The state line?" Cherry repeats, alarmed. "But—"

"It's safe now, Cherry." I pat her shoulder. "No worries."

Brad and Cherry help Renni into the backseat, as she's developed a limp, favoring her left knee either as a result of a zombie bite or Cherry's poor spatial judgment with the Jeep. They sit on either side of her, Brad pleasantly quiet, Cherry talking nonstop. Carmelle slips into the driver's seat, abandoning her rifle for the steering wheel and speeding us down the road, careful not to run over the bodies of the pseudo-zombies. Cherry explains to us how she finally met up with Carmelle, and how none of them felt right about leaving me behind, especially after hearing the news report and plans for burning out the city. The three of them went to the hospital and found the tunnels that led to the high school boiler room.

"We heard all this noise upstairs, but when we got up there no one was around," Cherry says. "It was really creepy. Also, hey, do you remember Randal Simmons from your fifth period English class in ninth grade? His picture's up in the case outside the principle's office; he's totally a senator now or something. Isn't that weird? Anyway, we got to the gym, and we found all these weapons and this Jeep, and Carmelle was like, we have to keep going, and so then we just drove, and then we heard all these, like, zombies moaning, and we just followed them, and there you guys were. Isn't that awesome? How everything worked out so well?"

I avoid looking at Renni in the rearview mirror as Carmelle releases the gearshift to take my hand. Carmelle smiles at me, and I smile at her. I try to explain about the pseudo-zombies and Nick Fury and how everything is okay now, at least as far as us being able to get out and not becoming zombies goes, but my words get muddled, and everyone just kind of accepts that they'll have to wait to fully understand.

We pull onto the main road, and I see taillights up ahead. Our convoy. As we near them, Carmelle slows down and shifts into first gear. She clears her throat, and licks her lips. "So, baby," she says to me. "In this time apart, I've had some time to think. And what I was thinking was.... Well, how do you feel about open relationships?"

This time, I let my eyes wander to the rearview mirror. I catch Renni's eyes there, and watch her lip curl up at the corner as she slips on her miraculously intact sunglasses. Being now well-versed in the facial quirks of Renni Ramirez, I return her smirk.

"I don't know, Carmelle. How do you feel about long-distance ones?"

The End

About the Author

Dayna Ingram grew up in Ohio and has since moved to the Bay Area, where she spends most of her time workin', schoolin', and forcin' her dog to wear sweater vests. For more info on her writing projects, visit thedingram.blogspot.com.

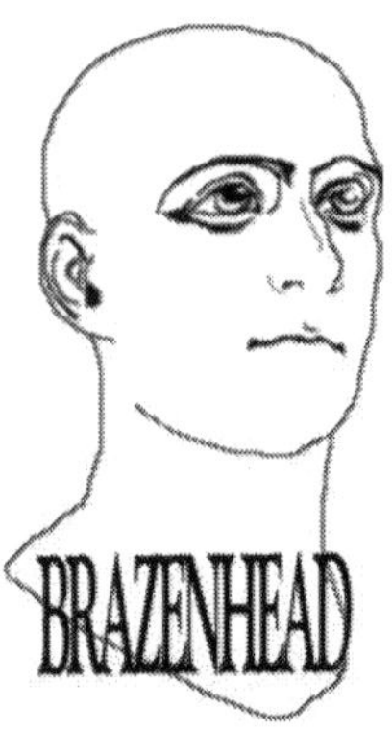

exceptional novellas of queer speculative fiction

No. 1: eat your heart out *by* Dayna Ingram (2011)

sentenceandparagraph.com/brazenhead
brazenhead@sentenceandparagraph.com